STAR TREK®
THE NEXT GENERATION

STAR TREK:
THE NEXT GENERATION NOVELS

STAR TREK:
THE NEXT GENERATION GIANT NOVELS

STAR TREK
THE NEXT GENERATION

PERCHANCE TO DREAM

HOWARD WEINSTEIN

TITAN BOOKS
LONDON

STAR TREK **THE NEXT GENERATION 19:**
PERCHANCE TO DREAM
ISBN 1 85286 412 5

Published by
Titan Books Ltd
19 Valentine Place
London SE1 8QH

First Titan Edition December 1991
10 9 8 7 6 5 4 3 2 1

British edition by arrangement with Pocket Books, a division of Simon
and Schuster, Inc., Under Exclusive Licence from Paramount Pictures
Corporation, The Trademark Owner.

Printed and bound in Great Britain by Cox and Wyman Ltd, Reading,
Berkshire.

For
Tom Roberts—
friend
and
teacher

Author's Notes

Twenty-five years!?

Wait a minute. How did twenty-five years go by so quickly? I was just this twelve-year-old kid watching "The City on the Edge of Forever" and "The Trouble with Tribbles" and "Journey to Babel"—

And suddenly, I'm . . . well, we don't really need to go into how old I am now, do we?

As I write this, we're celebrating the silver anniversary of a unique show biz/pop culture phenomenon— "Star Trek." The original cast appears in *Star Trek VI: The Undiscovered Country* in theaters, and the amazingly successful "Next Generation" is into its fifth season.

Like many of you, I've been a "Star Trek" fan pretty much since the beginning. By now, of course, the story of "Star Trek's" struggles to survive its early days has become legend—how NBC threatened to cancel the show after each of its first two seasons before finally pulling the plug after a disappointing third year . . . and how Star Trek snuck from its assigned grave under cover of rerun darkness, and rose on syndicated wings to a rebirth in movies and "Next Generation" reincarnation on television.

Whew . . . sounds kind of religious, huh?

Well, in considering "Star Trek's" amazing journey, I dug up an interesting artifact from my files (yeah, I'm a pack rat): a twenty-two-year-old note from NBC responding to my letter protesting "Star Trek's" final cancellation. I'll be kind and omit the name of the guy who signed it, but I wanted to share with you a paragraph from this historical footnote, dated June 5, 1969:

> "We too believe that 'Star Trek' is an attractive show with a fine cast. It was for these reasons that it found a spot in our schedule in the first place *but, unfortunately, the program failed to develop the broad appeal necessary for keeping it in our schedule next season.*" [My italics]

Uh-huh. I hereby nominate the above statement for the "Famous-Last-Words Hall of Fame," where it should take its place of honor alongside such utterances as "Are you kidding? They'll *love* the Edsel!" and "MTV? Who's gonna watch *music* on *televison?*" and "Don't worry about the tapes, Mr. Nixon— nobody'll *ever* find out about 'em."

In fairness, of course, nobody had any idea "Star Trek" would prove to be so durable. But it has, enriching countless lives in countless ways. For me, "Star Trek" is part of what made me want to become a writer; and many of my best friendships have grown out of my encounters with "Star Trek" and its fans.

So, a special silver-anniversary tip of the hat to some golden "Trek" friends and colleagues, without whom, as the saying goes, none of this would have been possible: Bob and Debbie Greenberger, Dave McDonnell and Starlog, Lynne Stephens, Joel and

Nancy Davis, Cindi Casby, the Burnside clan, Rich Kolker, Peter David, Sharon Jarvis and Joan Winston, Steve and Renee Wilson, Lance and Kathy Woods, the generous and dedicated committees of the Shore Leave, Clippercon, OktoberTrek and Fan-Out conventions, David Gerrold, Harlan Ellison, Ann Crispin, Dave and Kevin at Pocket Books . . . and *you*, the folks who've supported Star Trek and read these novels for all these years.

Here's to the next twenty-five—

Howard Weinstein
Autumn 1991

Chapter One

"JEAN-LUC, I DO *not* like being handcuffed."

Captain Picard sighed. "In what context, Dr. Crusher?" From the pugnacious thrust of her chin, it was quite clear that his chief medical officer had been mightily offended by someone or something. It was equally certain that Beverly Crusher had no intention of leaving Picard's ready room until she'd extracted a satisfactory response to her displeasure.

He folded his hands in priestly patience, knowing he wouldn't have to wait long for her to get to the specifics. Like gathering stormclouds, her eyebrows lowered into a frown. *Here it comes—*

"I don't like twiddling my thumbs while patients suffer—and I will not simply wait for someone else to cure them."

Picard motioned her to the couch across from his desk as he tried to deduce the source of her wrath.

It was only as she sat that the doctor noticed the tiny holographic solar system hovering over the captain's shoulder. At least three dozen objects darted, spun and whirled—planets, moons, random rocks and a squadron of tiny spacecraft. "What in heaven's name is that?"

"Hmm?" With a flicker of frustration in his eyes, he glanced at the cosmological chaos floating in the air. "Oh, just some blasted navigational puzzle that's been driving me to distraction for the past week. But I refuse to surrender. Computer, store puzzle for later reference." The hologram winked out of sight and Picard faced Crusher. "Would I be correct in guessing the cause of your indignation to be our orders to pick up those ten injured workers at the Chezrani outpost?"

"You would. By telling the *Enterprise* to get them and then rush them to a starbase hospital, Starfleet is as good as implying that the *Enterprise* is just some ambulance and the ship's medical staff are ambulance attendants."

"Doctor, I hardly think—"

"No one has ever been poisoned by processed ridmium particles before," she said, cutting him off. "There's nothing in the medical literature about effective treatment regimens."

"So you're saying these patients will not necessarily get better care at Starbase 96 than they might in your sickbay—?"

Crusher's fists clenched. "No. I'm saying I can do *more* for them on the *Enterprise*. The only thing we really know about ridmium is that it attacks the immune system."

"Ahh. And if I recall, research in immunology is one of your specialties."

"You recall correctly, Jean-Luc. And my medical staff is just as capable as any—"

"You are preaching to the choir," said Picard

calmly, hoping to deflect her anger. "It's going to take us approximately thirty-six hours to get from the Chezrani system to Starbase 96. I see no reason you shouldn't devote that time to developing an effective treatment."

Beverly did seem placated, a bit of the starch washed from her posture. "That's what I planned to do all along. I just wanted to make sure I had your support."

"You always have that. You know the high regard I have for your professional skills."

"I wish Starfleet shared that opinion," she pouted.

"I seriously doubt they view you as a glorified ambulance attendant."

"Who said anything about 'glorified,'" Crusher said, a flash of resentment in her eyes.

Picard rose and circled the desk, standing over her. "Beverly, they made you Chief of Starfleet Medicine. What greater compliment could they pay you?"

With a sigh, she slumped back against the couch cushion. "I guess you're right, Jean-Luc. Maybe I'm overreacting."

"I don't think this is the only thing on your mind."

The doctor managed a sliver of a smile. "Trespassing on Counselor Troi's turf?"

Picard smiled back. "Without Betazoid empathic powers, I would not even make the attempt. But we simple starship captains can also benefit from developing a certain sensitivity to the moods and concerns of crew members."

His oblique invitation to dump her troubles right there on his ready room desk was definitely tempting, but she waved it off with a shake of her head. "Oh, hell . . . you wouldn't understand, Jean Luc."

"Try me."

Beverly considered the offer, but remained mute. During the silence, Picard pondered the merits of continued persistence. He truly liked and respected Beverly Crusher, but he'd be the last to claim any clear comprehension of her inner workings. She could be mercurial, stiff-necked, skeptical—all matching the personality profile usually associated with redheads. But she was also much more than that simple profile. And exceedingly complex. Gaining firsthand knowledge of her personal demons might not be his wisest course.

Still, she was not only a trusted officer. She was also his friend. So much for wisdom, he concluded with a mental shrug. He was not going to let her leave without giving her every chance to unburden herself.

"I know you usually confide in Counselor Troi," he said. "Under the circumstances, I thought I might suffice for the moment. If I were to hazard a guess, I'd say you're worried about Wesley."

"Good lord—am I that transparent?" Crusher's expression softened into a wondering, gentle laugh. "It's so strange, Jean-Luc. When I took that Starfleet Medical assignment back on Earth, I worried about my son because I *didn't* know what he was doing or where he was. Then I came back to the *Enterprise,* and I started worrying about him because I *did* know what he was doing and where he was. When you're a mother, you just can't win."

"I understand better than you might think," Picard said with a twinkle as he perched on the edge of his desk.

"Hmm. I guess there is a maternal, nurturing component to being a starship captain." With a shake of her head, she got up and paced the small ready room. "I know Wesley's been on away teams before. I

4

keep telling myself that. But somehow it was different when the *Enterprise* was right there in planet orbit. This is the first time he's gone down to a planet and we've gone off to do something else."

"So you feel like you've abandoned him on Domarus Four?"

"I guess I do."

"Beverly, it's not like we dropped him naked and helpless," Picard scolded gently. "He's with two other capable Academy candidates, not to mention Data and Troi. And they do have a shuttlecraft."

Despite her best efforts to sidestep her gathering gloom, Beverly's expression darkened and her voice took on a momentary quaver. "I know that. I know that we're going to be rendezvousing with them in an hour or so. I also know that someday, he's going to be off on a ship of his own and I won't be able to keep an eye on him. And I *do* know that Wesley isn't Jack—" As soon as she'd said it, she was sorry.

The captain felt himself tense at the mention of Beverly's late husband, who'd died years ago under Picard's command. He hoped she wouldn't notice his reaction, but by the way her eyes looked away from his, he sensed her regret at having mentioned Jack's name. Was the source of that regret her natural reluctance to equate the father's fate with the son's future? Or was she sorry because she knew she'd inadvertently reminded Picard of his own feelings of responsibility and regret over Jack's death?

He couldn't be sure. But he was certain of this: no captain ever forgets the death of a comrade. Nobody knew that better than Beverly Crusher. Through her own grief, she'd seen the sorrow in Picard's eyes the day he brought Jack's body home. And as *Enterprise* chief medical officer, she'd seen the echoes of that

5

same sorrow every time she'd had to tell him a crew member had died.

When it came to Jack, though, they'd never completely sorted out their tangled feelings. It wasn't any great surprise, then, that throughout Beverly's years serving aboard Picard's starship, the ghost of Jack Crusher had been along for the voyage. For both of them.

She made a halfhearted attempt to erase the moment of revelation. "I didn't mean . . . oh, dammit, yes I *did.* I tell myself over and over that just because Jack died on a space mission doesn't mean my son will. But in here . . . " She brushed her hand across her heart. ". . . I can't convince myself of that."

"Beverly, sooner or later you'll have to let Wesley lead his own life."

"I know. And the closer that time comes, the more I want to push it back." She took a breath, not at all certain she wanted to pursue the matter. "Jean-Luc, can I ask you something personal?"

"Yes."

"When did you feel like your mother let you go?"

Picard suppressed a smile, but it lit his eyes. "Never."

Beverly Crusher winced. "Oh, wonderful . . ."

Shading his eyes with one hand, Wesley Crusher fended off the setting sun of Domarus Four as he peered toward the flattened crest of the mountain looming over him. She was up there somewhere, but he couldn't spot her. He wondered if she'd ducked back into one of those little caves pocking the flanks of the rugged mesa.

Gina Pace was forever charging headlong over,

through and under things and places that most people would approach with caution. Wes couldn't call her reckless. Not exactly, anyway. She just treated risk as something to be prepared for and dealt with, rather than a cause for alarm. As both Gina's friend and fellow Starfleet Academy candidate, Wes found her enthusiasm alternately amusing and exasperating.

Right at this moment, however, he was not amused. The gathering dusk had already tinged the sky with darkening splashes of purple and red, and this field trip was drawing to a close. They still had equipment and samples to stow on the shuttlecraft before they could head for orbit and rendezvous with the *Enterprise* on the Starship's return from a supply drop at the Nivlakan colonies two days distant.

The Starfleet chest insignia pinned to his uniform let out an electronic chirp, followed by a voice. "Commander Data to Ensign Crusher."

Wes tapped the communicator to reply. "Crusher here, sir."

"Are you returning to base camp?"

"Uhh—we're on our way, Commander. Crusher out."

Wes cupped his hands and bellowed up to where he'd last seen Gina. "Hey, Pace! Come down *now!*" He could have called her via communicator, but— what the hell—echoes were fun. Even at eighteen, and knowing the physics and acoustics involved, he still found a moment of childlike joy in hearing his own voice rebounding off cooperative rocks.

He squinted skyward again, just as Gina popped out of a cave entrance and clambered like a mountain goat down the steep slope. Loose pebbles skittered down ahead of her, but she never missed a step.

She hopped off a ledge and landed in front of Wesley. "I'm not late, am I? I just wanted to get a few more rock samples. *Amazing* formations up there! I couldn't leave without getting the best possible selection. If you were the captain and I was your science officer, wouldn't you want to *know* you could rely on me to do the best, most thorough job possible?"

She finally stopped for a breath, and he looked down at her, trying to maintain a gaze of Picard-like sternness—no easy task, since Gina was small and exceedingly cute, with large dark eyes, and he really wanted to run his fingers through her thick shaggy hair. He and Gina hadn't always gotten along. A few years ago, at fourteen, he'd been shy as a fieldmouse, and he thought she was loud and obnoxious. Then, at sixteen, when he felt ready for some tentative flirting, he thought she'd become a lot less childish. Now, at eighteen . . .

But this wasn't the time or place. He was her commanding officer on an important field excursion detail and he felt duty-bound to set an example. It took him a second to refocus his attention. *What did she just ask me? Oh, yeah . . .*

"Yes," he managed to say, finding his way back to the loose end of their conversation, "I'd want my science officer to be thorough. But I'd also like to know that I wouldn't have to worry about her getting lost or left behind because she went off on her own. Understood?"

"Understood." She narrowed her eyes, weighing the gravity of the moment. "I don't have to call you 'sir,' do I?"

"Nobody's keeping score. Let's get back to camp."

They began walking, quickly. Gina barely came up to Wesley's shoulder, and the height disadvantage forced her to jog just to keep up with his long-legged strides. "Where's Kenny?"

"I sent him back while I was looking for you," he said with a reproachful look.

"Oh. Y'know, I can't believe he wouldn't go into those caves with us."

"Some people prefer wide-open spaces."

"But Kenny *doesn't,*" she said with a derisive laugh. "He'd rather be on a space ship than a planet. Sometimes I just don't believe him. He can be so strange."

"He hates when you call him Kenny."

"And why would that be?" asked Gina with a defiant look that revealed her complete lack of patience for what she viewed as Kenny's eccentricities.

"He thinks it makes him sound like a little kid."

She shrugged. "Well, he acts like one sometimes."

"We all do sometimes," he said pointedly.

"So what does he want to be called, *Captain* Kenny?"

Wes grinned in spite of himself. "Just Ken, I think."

"I'll try to remember that."

The glint in her eyes made Wesley doubt her sincerity. As they approached the woods fringing the grassy plain which had been the object of most of their geology survey, Wes decided Domarus had been an interesting place for this field work. His satisfied judgment rested partly on the fact that it hadn't been just an academic exercise. Their performances would of course be evaluated by Data and Troi, and added to their Academy entrance application files. But the information they'd gathered would also enlarge the scanty file on a world which had been visited just once before, eighty years earlier.

The science vessel U.S.S. *Jonathan Levy,* one of the

most active exploration ships of its time, had done that original survey, but hadn't had the time to log more than a cursory orbital scan, including the geological and biological basics and the conclusion that Domarus Four hosted no sentient life forms, just lots of plants and smaller animals. Wes and his team hadn't found anything to contradict those reports, but it was fun just the same to do some adult work with minimal supervision.

Though he couldn't be certain, Wes had a feeling more and more these days that his time aboard the *Enterprise* was drawing to a close. Was it only three years ago that he'd failed the Starfleet Academy entrance exam? It seemed like a lot longer. As a scared fifteen-year-old, he'd been devastated by a failure. He believed he'd let down his mother, the captain, his friends, the entire ship—until Captain Picard had found him moping in the observation lounge and stunned him with a startling confession: "If it helps you to know this," Picard had said to him, "I failed my first time . . . and you may not tell anyone!"

Picard had also told him that a person's successes and failures could only be measured from within, not by anyone else but himself. Not an easy lesson to learn, but Wesley Crusher thought lately that he was finally beginning to understand it.

For reasons Wesley never quite understood, Picard had designated him an acting ensign, giving him access to experiences no Starfleet cadet could possibly have sitting in an earthbound classroom. Then, through a combination of natural talents and several tons of hard work, he'd achieved a field commission, earning his red ensign's uniform. He was a real starship officer.

After all that, he found it hard to imagine not being a member of the *Enterprise* crew. Would entering Starfleet Academy feel like a step backward? Maybe. But if he ever wanted to be even half the captain that Picard was, he knew he needed what the Academy had to offer, the theoretical foundation that would give perspective to practical experiences like this away-team mission.

Hiking over a grassy knoll, Wes and Gina entered a forest of towering, slender trees with golden leaves. En route, they found Ken Kolker hunched over like a stocky forest gnome, clipping and collecting some last-minute flora samples. All his classmates knew Ken as the most perpetually serious seventeen-year-old aboard the *Enterprise,* his moods often as dark as his close-cropped hair. As Wes gestured toward the clearing where the shuttle and their supervising officers waited, Ken fell into step.

But Gina stopped short. *"Dammit."*

Wes stopped, too, his hands on his hips and his mouth pinched into an expression of long-suffering impatience. "What did you forget to do now?"

"That stupid seismic testing rig—I forgot to shut it down," she said, already backing away. "I'll go back for it—I'll run—I'll—"

"I did it," said Ken, halting her in mid-stride.

Gina blinked at him. "You did *what—?"*

"On my way back here, I ran down the mission checklist on my tricorder and I noticed the rig wasn't checked off. So I figured I might as well—"

"Oh, you and your stupid checklists," Gina said with a roll of her eyes.

"Checklists are important," Ken huffed.

"There's more to life than checklists, *Kenny,"* she

11

said, emphasizing the dimunitive she now knew he disliked. "Do you ever do anything without consulting one of your stupid checklists first?"

"Gina," Wesley said sharply, "his checklist kept you from getting into trouble."

"Oh, Wes—that's not why he retrieved the seismic rig. He probably did it just to make me look bad."

Out of the corner of his eye, Wes saw how the accusation stung the shorter teen. No one who knew Ken would characterize him as the life of any party, and there was a germ of truth in Gina's opinion of his lack of spontaneity. But this jab was more than unfair. It was mean. "Gina, that's not—"

"Forget it, Wesley," Kenny said, gathering the remnants of his tattered dignity. With no intention of defending himself further, he turned and trudged toward the base camp.

Wes watched him go, then turned to glare down at Gina. "That was totally uncalled for. How do you think it would've looked if you suddenly remembered about that test rig after we'd closed the hatch and headed for orbit? You made a mistake—and then you made it worse. We're a team and team members are supposed to back each other up. That's all Ken was doing."

Gina looked away and scuffed the dirt with her toe. "You're mad at me."

"Yes, I am—but that's not the point."

"What is?"

"What do you think the point is?"

"Teamwork." She looked up at him. "Are you going to report me?"

He frowned, stretching the moment. *She really is cute . . .* "Nobody's perfect," he finally said, his tone softer.

"Not even you, Wes?" she teased.

"Especially not me."

"I guess I should apologize to Kenny."

"That's up to you."

Back at the away team's base camp, they found Ken kneeling in the shadow of the shuttle *Onizuka,* sorting his last batch of soil and plant samples into appropriate slots in a carrying case. As Gina approached him, Wesley busied himself just out of sight (but within earshot) on the shuttle's opposite side.

"If you came to make some comment on how compulsive I am," Ken said without looking up, "save it."

"Geez, you don't have to be so touchy. I just came over to apologize."

Ken's eyes flicked up in genuine surprise. "You did?"

Gina nodded. "I forgot we're a team." She peered over his shoulder, into a sample case awesome in its attention to total order and detail. "But you *are* the little compulsive, aren't you?" Delivered with a sly grin, her question was not meant as an insult—and Ken didn't take it that way.

"It's one of the few things I'm really good at," he answered with a slight smile.

She crouched for a closer look. "God, I wish I could be that neat. Then maybe I wouldn't always be losing or forgetting things."

"Creative people are allowed to be a little absent-minded."

Her brows hitched, detecting a compliment. "You think I'm creative?"

"Gina, everybody loves your artwork."

"What do you think of it?"

Ken shut the sample case and they both

straightened up. "I—uh—I'm the wrong person to ask. Some people are tonedeaf—"

"Oh, yeah, and you're art-impaired?" she scoffed. "Kenny, if you'd just have come into those caves with us—the way those minerals looked under our searchlamps—"

"Me? In a cave? No way—not where ceilings collapse and bury people!" he said with a shudder. Then he nodded skyward. "I'd much rather be up there in a ship, any ship."

"People die in space, too, y'know."

"Statistically, it's much safer to—"

"Oh, nooo—not statistics again," Gina moaned, covering her eyes with her hands and shaking her head. "What've you got against being on a planet?"

"I was born in space."

"On a ship?"

Now it was Kenny's turn to roll his eyes. "Of course on a ship. I was five before I even set foot on a planet."

"God . . . that's weird."

"Not as weird as you think. It just gives you a different perspective on things, that's all. To me, it's perfectly normal to be inside a contained, controlled, predictable environment."

Eavesdropping from the other side of the shuttlecraft, Wesley thought this sounded like a good time to take advantage of the truce between his friends, and he rejoined them. Under his supervision, they set about packing and stowing the last of the base-camp gear.

"This part is not fun," Gina grunted as she maneuvered a bulky equipment crate toward the squat craft.

"We're not here to have fun," Ken said. "We're gaining experience that'll up our chances of getting into the Academy."

14

"There's no regulation that says we can't have fun, too. Hey, Wesley, help me explain—"

"No way. I'm not getting in the middle of another one of your debates," Wes said with a grin as he scanned the area. "That's it. We're done."

As the three teens climbed through the shuttle's side hatch, none of them noticed the glittering scintilla flitting in the air above and behind them, at the edge of the clearing.

Commander Data and Counselor Deanna Troi greeted the young away team in the main cabin.

"Ready for departure, sir," Wesley said.

"Very good, Ensign," Data said pleasantly. "Mr. Kolker."

Ken had already moved to a seat in the back when the android's voice made him turn. "Yes, sir?"

"In view of your expressed interest in helm and navigation studies, I thought you might like to pilot the shuttle into orbit."

Kenny's round, somber face lit with excitement and his answer started to tumble out. "Pilot—? *Yessir—*" He caught himself in mid-sentence and wrestled his excess enthusiasm back under control, an embarrassed flush tinting his cheeks. "I mean, thank you, Commander. I would."

As he passed Gina on his way to the cockpit, she stifled a giggle. "Wouldn't want to have fun . . . nuh-uh . . . not cool Kolker."

Wes and Data followed Kenny into the front compartment, leaving Troi and Gina behind. The counselor looked at her young companion with knowing eyes. "I see you're still giving Ken a hard time."

"Ooo—he asks for it." Then Gina composed her gamine face into an expression of exaggerated dignity. "I know, I know—it's not mature."

"But sometimes you can't help it."

With a confessional shrug, Gina slid into the form-fit seat. "I bet you were perfect when you were my age."

A sly smile curled one corner of Deanna's mouth. "Mmm . . . my mother would dispute that appraisal," she said dryly.

"So, how did we do on this mission?"

"Gina, you know I can't tell you what your evaluations will be. Though it is just like you to ask."

"Scientists have to be inquisitive, right?"

They felt the shuttle rise off the planet surface, shimmying for a couple of unsteady moments, then smoothing out and banking off toward the Domaran sunset.

"Hmm," said Gina. "Not too bad for a rookie."

Kenny seemed right at home in the pilot's seat as he guided the small spacecraft toward standard orbit (though he hoped no one had noticed his slightly wobbly lift-off). Wesley sat beside him, handling sensors and support systems, while Data hovered just behind the two boys, keeping his supervisory presence to an unobtrusive minimum.

"Estimated time of arrival at rendezvous point," Data asked.

"Thirty-three minutes, sir," said Wesley.

"Maintaining course and speed," Ken said.

Wesley gave his scanners a cursory glance, then frowned as he noticed something unusual. "Commander, there's a ship approaching planet orbit."

"Is that the *Enterprise* arriving ahead of schedule?"

"No, sir, not the *Enterprise.* Unfamiliar configuration, with no identification beacon."

The android leaned over Wesley's shoulder for a

look. "Hmm. Most curious." He activated the communications system. "Federation shuttle *Onizuka* to unidentified vessel. We are on a science survey mission—our presence is nonhostile. Please state the purpose of your approach."

Awaiting a reply, Data punched up a magnified image of the approaching vessel on the main viewer. Ungainly in design, it was roughly the same size as the *Enterprise,* and apparently scarred by both battle and wear.

"Looks like she's seen better days," Wes murmured.

Data repeated his message—again, without verbal response. The alien vessel held its heading, leaving very little doubt that its convergence with the tiny shuttlecraft was not coincidental.

"Mr. Kolker," Data said calmly, "evasive maneuver—come to course one-two-five mark nine."

For a long moment, Ken sat frozen. Wes glanced over and saw the younger boy chewing his lip anxiously. "Kenny—"

At Wesley's prompt, Ken's fingers skipped across his panel, entering Data's instructions flawlessly. Out in space, the unidentified ship altered course, clearly bent on interception.

"We may be nonhostile," Wes said nervously, "but I'm not so sure about them."

Without warning, a tractor beam leapt from the silent intruder, crossing the void and snaring the shuttlecraft in a pulsing golden haze. The *Onizuka* immediately shook in protest, shuddering down to its rivets.

Kenny went pale, tightening his panicky grip on the edges of his control panel.

Wes Crusher swallowed hard, trying to moisten a mouth suddenly gone dry and pasty. "Commander, that tractor beam is too intense. If it keeps up, we're going to break apart."

Data peered at the sensor readout. "I concur," he said, his tone as mild and dispassionate as usual.

Wesley spun around and stared into the android's wide yellow eyes. For all his intentions of setting an example for the other kids and being the brave young Starfleet officer, Wes was an eighteen-year-old scared to the bone. Fear widened his eyes and spiked into his voice. *"Data*—what do we *do?"*

Whatever Data decided, Wes knew it had to be soon—and it *better* be right.

Chapter Two

IN THIS CASE, the vast repository of knowledge nested within Data's positronic brain was as good as a dry hole. The tractor beam gripping the shuttlecraft was simply too powerful; escape was impossible, as clearly demonstrated by a brief and futile attempt which succeeded only in straining the engines to the point where the shuttle's computer automatically throttled them back to prevent critical damage.

Only one option remained. Data opened a communications channel. "Shuttle *Onizuka* to unidentified vessel. Please reduce the intensity of your tractor beam. If you scan us, you will find that your beam will cause the destruction of this craft within seventy-three seconds." Then he switched frequencies. *"Onizuka* to *Enterprise.* We have been trapped in Domaran orbit by an unidentified starship. We—"

"No good, Data," said Wesley with a frustrated shake of his head. "Our subspace signal can't get through this energy field. Should we prepare to launch an emergency message capsule?"

Data's brows frowned slightly. "It is unlikely that a message capsule could escape the gravitational field of the intruder's tractor beam." Then he brightened, without noticing the disheartening effect of his next observation on Wesley and Ken. "Then again, due to its structural design, a message capsule might possibly survive if the shuttlecraft is destroyed, thus leaving an account for the *Enterprise* when it arrives. An excellent suggestion, Wesley. Encode all relevant information."

Wes stared at the android for a disbelieving moment. Unfortunately, this wasn't the proper time to coach Data on the relevance of human feelings in a crisis; but he made a mental note to mention it later—if they got out of this. Instead, he said, "Yes, sir," with a weak nod and his fingers skipped across his keypad.

"Commander, look," Kenny said, pointing to the sensor readout.

Data peered at the display screen, pleased at what he saw. "Ahh. They have reduced their beam intensity by forty percent. We are no longer in imminent danger."

"Message capsule ready," Wesley said.

"Launch it, Ensign."

Wesley keyed the computer and they heard a sound like a sigh from the shuttle's belly. The tiny capsule popped out of its storage niche and streaked away. But Data had been right; it wasn't able to break free of the tractor beam. Held within the narrow channel of the beam, it managed to go about two hundred meters—

—where a pinpoint phaser burst from the alien ship blasted it into a puff of dust.

"Dammit," Wesley growled, thumping his fist against the arm of his seat.

"Most unfortunate," Data said. "That was our only chance to report our predicament to the *Enterprise* or any other vessels that might enter this area."

"We won't be at the rendezvous," Ken whispered. "They'll never find us—"

"Of course they will," said Wesley.

"Not if we don't exist anymore," Ken countered in a jittery voice.

With strong hands, Data swiveled both their seats to face him. "Debating our eventual disposition is not the best use of our—"

"Federation shuttle," a harsh female voice said from the comm speaker. There was no doubting the authority it carried. "This is the *Glin-Kale,* flagship of the Teniran Echelon. We are claiming this world. You are guilty of trespass in our territory. You will be held as prisoners—until we decide your fate."

"I guess it's a little like a horse with a loose rein," Beverly Crusher said as her own horse, a well-muscled chestnut mare, ambled along the sun-dappled trail, choosing its own easy pace and pausing now to graze on a stand of tall grass waving in a spring-scented breeze.

"What is?" Picard called as he trotted up on his white Arabian. Picard's horse stopped alongside hers to sample the grass.

"Fate, Jean-Luc."

He contemplated the analogy for a moment. "I see what you mean. It can meander calmly, or break into a gallop without warning—"

"Leaving you to hang on for dear life." She was rather pleased with the analogy.

"There's a difference, though," Picard said, affectionately patting his horse's neck. "A competent rider has the means to control his mount, where Fate simply refuses to be broken to the saddle . . . if you believe in Fate at all."

Beverly shrugged. "I'm still open on that question." With a sure but gentle touch, she reined her horse back to the trail, damp with morning dew. Picard fell into step beside her and she closed her eyes, letting the sunbeams streaming through the trees warm her face. "This ride was a wonderful idea, Jean-Luc. Just what I needed to relax before we pick up those injured workers at Chezrani. Thanks for suggesting it."

"Not at all," Picard said as the path led them up a gentle hillside. "There are times I prefer riding alone. It's a superb way to either concentrate on problems— or to forget them for a while, if that's the goal. But there are other times that call for companionship. Care to pick up the pace and trot a bit?"

Crusher gave him a dubious glance. "Uhh, I think I've had enough trotting and posting for one day. My thigh muscles are telling me it's been a *long* time since my college riding days."

"You're just out of practice. We should ride together more often."

"We should—but who has the time?"

The horses reached the top of the hill, where the wooded trail opened onto a broad green meadow splashed with colorful wildflowers. As the riders started across, Picard spotted a sturdy stone wall as high as his horse's head.

Beverly noticed the gleam in her captain's eye. "Jean-Luc, tell me you're not thinking of jumping that . . ."

"Why not?"

"My medical advice is, let's go around it."

"Nonsense. Are we the sort of people who skirt challenges?"

"Are we the sort of people who like broken bones?"

"Beverly, we can clear that wall."

"Unless you're giving us a direct order, Captain, my horse and I respectfully decline."

"Suit yourself." Picard turned his Arabian and, with an almost imperceptible signal from his boot heels, an indication of the rapport between man and beast, the horse dashed for the country wall.

"Jean-Luc—wait!"

"See you on the other side," Picard shouted back over his shoulder.

With a series of kicks not at all gentle, Beverly jolted her mare to a full gallop, trying to catch up. If she couldn't stop him, she at least wanted to be close at hand just in case . . . *oh, don't even think it . . .*

Picard and his horse were like one melded life-form, moving in perfect, powerful rhythm, racing toward the wall.

Ohmygosh, Beverly thought, *that wall's twelve feet if it's an inch . . . he'll never make it.* Shrinking distance and top speed meant Picard had only a matter of moments to change course, or stop.

And then those moments were gone. Had she had the presence of mind to think about it, Beverly would have remembered that the holodeck's primary programming included an array of safety factors that all but precluded serious injuries. If a lunatic chose to run headfirst into a stone wall, the wall would change at the last possible instant into an impact-absorbing cushion.

But here and now, the thundering of hooves overwhelmed such rationality. And she wanted only to close her eyes so she wouldn't see Picard and the Arabian crash against the unyielding obstacle. But she had to watch. If he made it, she had to *see* it. And if he didn't, she had to be ready.

The Arabian jumped, hooves slicing through the air, reaching for blue sky. Picard hunched forward, precisely balanced.

Beverly pulled back on her own reins and her horse skidded to a stop. *Fly, Jean-Luc, fly!*

They cleared the top stones, and they were over and out of sight.

But the sounds that immediately followed were wrong. Instead of triumphant hoofbeats continuing on the other side, Beverly heard a splashing skid, the alarmed whinny of a horse suddenly losing control of his own feet, and the terrible thud of a half-ton of horseflesh taking a tumble.

"Jean-Luc!"

Frantically, Beverly searched for the fastest way to get to Picard. Twenty meters down from where Picard had jumped, the stone wall blended into a much lower hedge. She could see grass on the other side, with plenty of room for a safe landing. She hunkered down in her saddle, wheeled the chestnut mare and charged the hedge, taking it in an easy leap.

Then she turned, stopped and gaped. In the shadow of the wall, the Arabian stood sheepishly, no longer white but spattered with viscous brown glop. And Jean-Luc Picard sat, legs splayed unceremoniously, in a pool of fresh, wet mud.

"Merde," he said.

Trying not to laugh, the doctor approached. "No— *mud."*

Picard's brow twitched. "Very funny."

"Are you hurt?"

"Only my dignity. By the way, excellent form on your jump."

"Yours, too—even though you'd lose a lot of points for your landing, Jean-Luc."

The chirp of the intercom interrupted their equestrian analysis and they heard First Officer Riker's voice. "Captain, we've got a problem."

Picard got to his feet. "What is it, Number One?"

"We're approaching the rendezvous point—but there's no sign of the shuttlecraft."

Picard glanced at Beverly, whose face went ashen. "Nothing on long-range scans?"

"No, sir. No communications contract, no message pods, no shuttle, no debris. Nothing at all."

"Are we within communications range of Domarus Four?"

"Yes, sir," said Riker. "We tried. No response. Of course, it could be nothing more than a malfunction in the shuttle's comm system. They might have stayed on Domarus Four to make repairs."

"Let's find out," Picard said as he snared his horse's loose rein and headed for the holodeck exit. "Set course for the Domaran system, warp six. And maintain attempts to locate the shuttle. I'll be on the bridge in five minutes. Picard out."

Like a beetle caught in a spider's web, the shuttle hung helplessly in the glow of the Teniran tractor beam. Inside, Troi, Data and the three teens waited. They could do little else.

"It's been twenty minutes," Wesley said, still seated next to Kenny in the cockpit command seats. "I wish they'd *do* something already."

"Like what?" Ken asked.

"I don't know . . . *anything*. I just hate waiting for the other shoe."

Data cocked his head. "What other shoe?"

"For the other shoe to *drop*."

"That would imply an initial shoe has dropped. Am I missing something?"

"It's an old Earth expression, Data," Wesley said.

With a batting of his eyelids, Data accessed the reference in his linguistics bank. "Ahh, yes. Connoting impatience, dread of impending events, foreshadowings of doom—" The android stopped when he noticed Ken and Wesley exchanging wan glances. "Shall I continue?"

"I don't think so, sir," Wes replied politely. He took a breath and exhaled slowly. "The *Enterprise* should come looking for us anytime now once they don't find us at the rendezvous point. Then the Tenirans'll have to make some kind of move."

"They'll have to let us go," Ken murmured.

"Not necessarily," Data said. As if on cue, both Wes and Kenny turned with pained looks on their faces, but Data continued. "They may retain us as a bargaining chip. They may even destroy us. Since we do not know their true motivations for capturing us, we cannot predict how they will react when confronted by a starship. Such a threat to—"

An alert chime interrupted him and Wes spun back to his console. "They're probing us—some kind of—"

Before Wesley could finish his sentence, the shuttle's instrument panels erupted in a hissing shower of sparks and smoke. Cabin lights dimmed and display screens blanked. Data reacted almost instantly, already reaching for circuit cut-offs as he spoke: "Their scanners are overloading our systems. Implement emergency shutdown procedures, now."

As quickly as they could, Wesley and Ken scrambled to save whatever systems they could from irreparable damage. With six hands tackling the task, they were done in a few seconds; then they sat bathed in the dim red glow of emergency lighting, the cabin eerily silent except for the quick, shallow breathing of two frazzled teenagers.

"The scanning beam is gone," Wes finally said.

"Status report, Ensign," Data said.

Wes powered up a small auxiliary computer screen and called up a systems check. "Primary computer down . . . main engines, navigation, communications and life support all out."

Data stepped over to a keypad set into the cockpit's aft bulkhead and entered a rapid series of reset commands. In response, a few instruments on the main consoles flickered back to life, and the distant hum of vent blowers provided some welcome background noise as they began clearing the acrid smoke of scorched electronics from the cabin.

"There," said Data. "Back-up life-support and computer systems are rerouted and functional. Let us see what other systems might be repaired."

Wesley swiveled out of his seat and squatted down to remove console access panels, but Ken remained motionless in his seat, frozen by fear. "Come on, Ken," Wes said gently as he crouched next to him. "You aced our last systems analysis lab. We can't untangle this mess without you."

After a long moment and several deep breaths, Kenny nodded and joined in the work.

* * *

As the starship *Enterprise* slowed and dropped out of warp speed, Picard sat back in his command seat and considered the image of Domarus Four growing on the bridge viewscreen. It looked very much like Earth in the proportions of its surface divided between scattered continents and blue oceans, with delicate ribbons of white clouds wrapped around it. In fact, it appeared quite benign, though Picard knew as well as anyone that planetary looks could certainly deceive.

But nothing in the original survey of Domarus—nor in the sensor sweep done by the *Enterprise* before dispatching the trainee away team—contradicted that evaluation. The field excursion led by Commander Data was designed to be as risk-free as possible. So what could have happened to prevent the shuttle's arrival at the planned rendezvous?

"Captain," Lieutenant Worf said from the Tactical console, "sensors have detected the shuttle in Domaran orbit . . ."

"Ahh, good."

". . . and a second vessel almost the size of this ship. It has the *Onizuka* trapped in a tractor beam."

First Officer Riker rose from his seat next to the captain. "Worf, scan the shuttle for life signs."

"Already scanned, sir. I read four humanoids and Data. But their comm system appears to be nonfunctional." The Klingon security chief scowled. "That tractor beam is interfering with our scanners—I cannot get a clear reading on the shuttle's overall condition."

"A closer look, Captain?" said Riker.

"Approach with caution, Number One. We don't want to startle whoever is holding the shuttle."

Riker nodded. "Lieutenant Worf, yellow alert," he

28

said as he stepped up behind the young blond woman seated at the conn station usually occupied by Wesley. "Ensign Burnside-Clapp, take us into orbit, slow and easy—fifty-thousand kilometer perigee."

The *Enterprise* slipped into high orbit on a trajectory calculated to keep it hidden behind Domarus, then made a stately approach toward the alien vessel and the tiny shuttle in its grip. Picard wanted to let the alien commander know the *Enterprise* was here without causing undue alarm.

As the other two ships came into view, the captain straightened in his seat. "Hold relative position. Any identification, Mr. Worf?"

"Negative, sir."

"Well, they know we're here," Riker said, "and they've made no attempt to contact us?"

"None," said Worf.

"Hmm." Captain Picard stood and joined his first officer under the bridge's central dome. "Your assessment, Number One?"

"Whoever they are, they must've been pretty nervous about something to feel so threatened by an unarmed shuttlecraft that they had to put a stranglehold on it."

"Then imagine the potential effect of our arrival."

Riker nodded. "Kid-glove treatment would seem to be in order."

"Agreed. Mr. Worf, open hailing frequency."

"Open, sir."

Picard and Riker both returned to their seats. "This is the U.S.S. *Enterprise,* Captain Picard commanding. We ask that you identify yourself and your mission." He waited a few moments for a reply. When none came, he repeated his greeting. "Please explain your presence in—"

A harsh female voice cut him off. "This is Captain Arit, commanding the *Glin-Kale,* flagship of the Teniran Echelon. Keep your distance, *Enterprise*—or we will destroy your shuttle."

"Captain Picard," Worf said in a low rumble, "additional sensor data—"

"Mute signal. What is it, Worf?"

"The shuttle has been damaged by the Teniran energy beam. All main systems out—back-ups may be failing as well."

Picard got to his feet, determined to settle this confrontation quickly. "Open channel. Captain Arit, your actions are endangering the crew of our shuttlecraft. Please release it."

"We claim this world for the Teniran Echelon, Picard. You and your shuttle are violating Teniran space."

"The Federation has no claims on Domarus Four," Picard said, his voice carefully balanced between calm and firm. "If it is indeed uninhabited, then we have no quarrel with your claim."

"This world is already ours."

"That subject can be debated *after* you release our shuttle."

"There is no debate, Picard."

Captain Picard did not like the brittle tone of his counterpart's announcement. "Mute signal."

"I suggest beaming our people out of there," said Riker.

Worf consulted his display screen, then shook his head. "Impossible, Commander. The tractor beam will interfere with our transporter signal."

Geordi La Forge turned from his engineering nook. "We could try to recalibrate for a one-shot beam-out, but it'll take time."

"We do not have time," Worf suddenly said, glaring down at his console. "The Tenirans just increased tractor intensity by eighty percent. The shuttle cannot withstand the stress for longer than ninety seconds."

"Damn," Picard muttered, still facing Worf and Geordi, his back to the main viewscreen. "Channel open. Captain Arit, your aggressive action is unacceptable. Release the shuttle immediately or we will be forced to—"

"What the hell is *that?*" Geordi muttered, taking a stride forward, staring across the bridge at the viewscreen.

Picard and Riker whirled just in time to see a splash of skittering colors surrounding the little shuttlecraft. The gaseous tendrils sliced right through the Teniran energy beam and seemed to tenderly caress the endangered *Onizuka* like sinuous fingers. Their colors blended and bled with such rapid fluidity that human eyes could not be sure what colors they'd seen.

Then the shuttle began to sparkle and fade, turning translucent.

"What's happening?" Picard demanded.

Before anyone on the *Enterprise* bridge could answer, the shuttle dissolved in a rainbow blaze of sparkling hues—*and vanished without a trace.*

Chapter Three

As PICARD GAPED at the viewer, he felt a queasy shudder in the pit of his stomach, as if he'd just been shoved off a precipice into free-fall. *What the hell happened to the shuttlecraft?*

But reflexes honed by long years of command took hold and he forced the stunned expression off his face. "Mr. Worf, report."

Worf seemed to be groping for a reply. "It is . . . simply gone, Captain. There is no correlation to this phenomenon in our data banks."

Picard responded with a nod. "Add visual to our signal. If the Tenirans respond in kind, put it on screen."

"Aye, sir," Worf said.

"Captain Arit," Picard boomed, "the unwarranted destruction of our shuttlecraft is an act of war."

The bland blue globe of Domarus Four left the main viewscreen, and Picard got his first look at the face of his adversary.

"We did nothing to your shuttle," Captain Arit said flatly, flashing small but noticeable fangs not quite hidden under full golden lips. Her large eyes, tinted a faint green, betrayed no fear—no emotion at all.

Picard had never seen a Teniran before, neither in the flesh nor in pictures, not even in passing. He would have remembered beings embodying such savage beauty. Momentarily mesmerized by Arit's tawny complexion and the rich black mane circling the delicate contours of her face, he wondered whether her appearance was typical of her species. Then he noticed the ragged quilting of her uniform, with fraying around the collar and an unmended rip at the shoulder seam. *A flagship commander wearing tattered hand-me-downs . . . ?*

"Then what happened to it?"

"That is your problem, Picard. Be out of Teniran space within one of your hours. Arit out." Her face disappeared from the viewscreen.

"That was a grave mistake, Captain Arit."

Arit winced at the sharp words from the pinched voice behind her. She didn't want to deal with this, not now. If she ignored him, didn't turn at all, maybe he'd just disappear from her bridge. Maybe—

"Why wasn't I *consulted?"*

He wouldn't disappear and she knew it. He never did, so why should this situation be any different. She would have to deal with him.

"Consulted about what, Egin?" With a grudging swivel of her chair, she faced the aging official. Egin's clenched fists rested on his hips in what Arit had long since accepted as a more or less permanent stance of aggressive impatience. His ill-fitting doublet stretched across his ample girth, and she found herself wondering whether the faded garment might just surrender to structural stresses and spontaneously pop apart.

"You know damn well what, Captain. You may command this ship, but *I'm* the First Valend of our government and I should have been consulted on your dealings with the *Enterprise.*"

"Egin, you're First Valend by default. You're the only Valend left—and I don't have to consult you on matters pertaining to the running of the *Glin-Kale.*"

Egin's head shook vigorously, setting a wispy mane of silver hair fluttering as his jowls quivered. "You can't just dismiss my authority like—"

She cut him off. "I'm tired of this argument, Egin. I was tired of it the first time we had it, and the hundredth time and the thousandth time."

His pursed mouth clamped shut for a longer than expected interval, but he wasn't ready to retreat. "Fine. Then I'll just state my case. We should have told this Picard that we had his shuttle and crewmen —it would have been the perfect bargaining trade-off."

Arit couldn't quite believe what she was hearing. Forget the fact that this starship *Enterprise* looked like a gleaming example of the Federation's finest— dismiss the likelihood that its sensors could probably have probed to the core of her own vessel. Could Egin really have failed to grasp the meaning of his own words? *Trade-off* implied that you actually had something to trade—or the strength to back up a bluff. She stared at him. "And what would've happened when they discovered we were lying?"

That shut him up. And to her astonishment, he turned smartly on one worn boot heel and marched off the bridge as if he'd been the victor. She muttered a disbelieving oath to herself, marveling at Egin's unflagging ability to fail to think any strategy through to its most obvious conclusion. No wonder he's spent his entire thirty-year career on the Council of Valends mired in the nether depths of government hierarchy. His colleagues must have perceived him for what he was—a drudge, stunningly limited in scope, though with a few political uses.

And now, in what Arit saw as one of the great cosmic jokes of all time, fate had spared Egin and taken him to heights even he had never imagined himself occupying. *If only I could see the humor in this particular joke . . .*

"Was the shuttlecraft destroyed, or was it *not?"* Jean-Luc Picard tried to keep the testiness out of his voice, but failed.

As Picard's words hung in the air, he glanced around the conference-room table at Riker, Worf and Geordi. No one seemed anxious to break the uncomfortable silence, but the burly Klingon spoke up first.

"If so, then it was disintegrated more completely than is possible with any weapon—or weapon *theory* —known to us."

Picard rubbed his chin and leaned back in his chair, certain that Worf's stark observation would stimulate the discussion. "Hmm . . . Please elaborate, Lieutenant."

"There was no explosion, no debris—not even the residual particles left after an object is destroyed by our phasers."

"If the Tenirans do have some unknown weapon," Riker said, "then they're a clear danger not only to this ship but to the entire Federation. And if they've got more ships like this one . . ."

Geordi shook his head. "I don't think it was a weapon. And I don't think the shuttle was destroyed."

Everyone stared at the chief engineer. They obviously wanted to agree with his statement, but their experience tempered that desire with skepticism. "Then what happened to it?" Riker asked.

"I think it was transported, for lack of a better term—and, pleasant as they are, I don't think the Tenirans had anything to do with it."

"Transported?" Riker repeated, his face pinched into a doubtful squint. "How and where?"

"I'm not sure how . . . and I don't know where."

"Mr. La Forge," Picard said, "I've never known you to make wild guesses."

"And I'm not making 'em now, Captain. Not entirely, anyway."

"Geordi, if you're not guessing," Riker said, "then what are you basing this on?"

The chief engineer clasped his hands and his gaze drifted across the table toward the observation windows. "Something weird that showed up in sensor analyses. Those swirling colors around the shuttle—? They were the visible result of strange energy patterns converging right around the shuttle."

Picard leaned forward, the intensity of his interest glittering in his eyes. "Energy patterns?"

"Yes, sir, and they were incredibly diffused. Once these energy patterns reached their target—the shuttlecraft—they coalesced into those swirling colors we saw."

"And you are saying that this diffused energy didn't come from the Teniran ship?" Picard asked.

"Yes, sir. I'm about ninety-five percent certain it came from the planet."

36

Riker thumped his fist on the table. "Then we should be able to pinpoint a source."

"I wish," Geordi sighed. "I already looked for residual energy readings down there—anything tell-tale. The energy patterns did not originate from one spot."

"Yet," Picard said, "you are still certain they did in fact come from the Domaran surface?"

"Positive, sir. I've ordered up continuous intensive scanning of the planet. If there's anything at all to be found down there—either some weird power source or the shuttle—we'll find it."

The captain frowned. "I wonder what else we might find . . ."

Arit sat in her dimly lit cabin, her jacket open to reveal a threadbare undervest beneath. She stared at the wide-bottomed bottle in her hand, her fingers wrapped firmly around its tapered neck. Did it hold answers, or merely escape? And what did that matter anyway? She liked the way the purple wine tasted, savored its fire as it went down. She felt so little these days—at least the burning in her belly reminded her she was still alive.

But the sensation was fleeting. Arit knew the truth. She was dying a lingering death. They all were. And she didn't really believe this place, this Domarus, would be their salvation.

"The *peroheen* again?" a gravelly voice scolded from behind her.

Arit turned slightly to see a familiar portly silhouette in the doorway where the hatch was stuck half-open. "You're not my mother, Jevlin."

"No, I'm your first officer, and I never should've let you take that case of *peroheen* when we—"

"A last reminder of home. Come in and join me, or go away and leave me alone. But please—don't stand there lecturing me."

"I'm not lecturing, Cap'n." He limped into the cramped cabin, leaning on a stout walking stick and dragging his gimpy right leg. "I've been more intimate with more bottles than you'll ever see. You can bet your life on that."

She poured the purple liquid into an extra glass and pushed it across the desk as Jevlin lowered his bulk into a chair. He shoved the glass back at her.

"Suit yourself," she said, adding the rejected drink to her own nearly empty glass. "There's nothing more dull than a reformed drunk." Then she downed half the combination in several continuous gulps.

"I could try to fix that," Jevlin said, wagging his thumb back toward the inoperative hatch.

"Fix what—being dull or being a reformed drunk?" Arit peered over the rim of her glass, wondering if she'd ever live to be as old and fat and gray as Jevlin.

"The door," he said sourly.

"Oh." She shrugged, honestly not caring. Somehow, it seemed harder and harder to care about much of anything these days, much less a broken door mechanism. "Why bother? It's been like that for months."

"A ship's cap'n needs privacy sometimes."

"On this ship?" She gave a skeptical snort. "Besides, I think of my hatch as the perfect symbol of everything else that doesn't work on the glorious old *Glin-Kale.*"

Jevlin seemed offended. "That's not fair, Cap'n. She's got us this far. She's got some heart left."

"The *Enterprise* may take care of that."

"We'll work things out," he said with a grin that

38

showed his chipped fangs. "But nobody's going to help us, Cap'n, nobody at all. It's up to us."

"You should've been on the bridge to see Egin in action this time."

"I heard."

Arit rubbed her eyes. She seemed to be tired most of the time these days. She still managed to sleep at night, but she couldn't recall the last time she'd awakened feeling rested. "I don't know why, but Egin's stupidity still astonishes me. Has it occurred to you that if we get through this, he'll have the same authority as Gansheya had? She was brilliant, and he's a turd."

Jevlin nodded. "Not quite fair that he's the only one who survived to make it this far. Who knows, Cap'n . . . anything could still happen."

"Ever the optimist. Have you got your little *shleeyah* with you?"

He patted the breast pocket of his shabby coat. "You know I'm never without it since it replaced the wine."

"Then play me a song, Jev." Arit closed her eyes and took a pensive sip of her wine.

"Any special song?" Jevlin asked as he slid the small instrument out of his pocket. The *shleeyah* was a black, flute-like tube about the size of his thumb, and he buffed it against his sleeve until it glinted in the glow of the desk lamp.

"First officer's discretion," she said with a hazy smile softened by the wine.

His hands were stubby and roughened by a life of hard labor, but his fingers cradled the instrument with a tenderness reserved for the touch of a lover's hand. He raised it to his lips and breathed into the slender mouthpiece; inside the cylinder, his warm breath blended into music and came out as a lilting tune that broadened the smile on Captain Arit's face.

As she listened to Jevlin's space chantey, she gazed out through the large square viewport over her bed. And she wondered what happened to that little shuttlecraft. She'd never intended to do any damage to the tiny defenseless ship, or harm those aboard it. But she'd learned the hard way that a little bluster up front could save a lot of scrambling for cover later on. And her strategy had indeed been working—until the *Enterprise* arrived. One look at that gleaming starship, and she knew there'd be no way for the old *Glin-Kale* to outgun her. But she'd still been willing to play out her hand. She'd have retained control over that shuttle only as long as it kept the *Enterprise* at bay. Then she'd have released it. A simple enough plan, ruined by . . . by what? Arit fervently wished she had the answer to that question.

Arit hated the unknown. She hated losing control. And she found herself driven by the simplest of yearnings—to feel a planet surface beneath her feet instead of metal decking, to breathe the fresh scent of a free-blowing breeze instead of the stale air recirculated through filters long since shot to hell. This planet, this Domarus Four, had appeared to be the answer to prayers—

But no longer. The way things were going, it might yet turn out to be the graveyard of what remained of the Teniran people.

The hour she'd given Picard would soon be up. Whatever happened, she knew she could not back down now.

"Your shuttle is gone, Picard," Arit said from the small viewscreen atop Picard's ready room desk.

40

"Permission to intrude on Teniran space is now rescinded. The *Enterprise* must depart immediately."

Picard sat at the desk with his hands folded, his face tranquil. "We have reason to believe our missing shuttlecraft has been transported down to Domarus Four and we—"

"Transported—? By *what?* You admitted yourself that Federation surveys classify this world as uninhabited by sentient life."

"Surveys can be incomplete, or wrong. We will not leave this system until we can be certain that our missing crew members are not somewhere down there on Domarus Four."

"Down there laying claim to our planet!" Arit said explosively.

"If Domarus does have native sentient life-forms," Picard countered, "then it is not your planet—"

"That is between us and these theoretical life-forms of yours. It is none of the Federation's business. I'm warning you, Picard—we will defend our territory."

"Why is the Teniran Echelon so interested in this particular planet?"

"That is none of your business either. Arit out."

The screen went abruptly blank, leaving Picard to swallow his next sentence. "Blast," he muttered, then turned toward Dr. Crusher, who'd been sitting across from him during the whole exchange. "Not my best diplomatic work."

Beverly managed a sympathetic smile. "She wasn't exactly receptive."

"I'm baffled by this intense desire to possess a world of no great value. What do you make of it, Doctor?"

"I'm not Deanna, Captain."

"I don't expect Betazoid empathic powers," he said kindly. "But I value your observations all the same."

41

Beverly frowned as she tried to make sense of what they'd heard from the Teniran commander. "Well . . . it was pretty obvious that Captain Arit is hiding the reasons why the Tenirans are so interested in Domarus. She seemed afraid of something."

Picard nodded. "I agree. But afraid of what? Of us?"

Crusher's brow creased thoughtfully. "I can't put my finger on it, but I think it's more than just us."

"Some unseen adversary, perhaps."

She shrugged. "I wish I knew . . ."

As her voice trailed off, Picard saw the worry in her eyes, and knew the rest of her unspoken thought—*I wish I knew what's happened to my son.*

"Thanks for your help, Beverly," he said as she got up.

"I'd better be getting back to the lab. We're starting to make some real progress on this ridmium poisoning case."

"Oh? That will be good news for the Chezrani accident survivors. Keep me posted." As he watched her leave, Picard wondered if this medical challenge would provide a much needed distraction for his chief surgeon, forcing her to think about something other than Wesley and the missing away team. Perhaps, but he knew such distractions were only momentary at best.

Left alone, Picard combed through the computer for all available scraps of information on the Tenirans. Unfortunately, there wasn't much to find. The Teniran homeworld was located far from any Federation systems, and contacts had been limited to sporadic trade. Beyond that, there were few specifics. No record of how many planets or outposts were counted as part of the Teniran Echelon. No historical background. Nothing to give Picard even the slightest hint of what might have brought this one Teniran vessel to an unprepossessing planet so far from home, and what could have compelled its captain to bully a defenseless shuttlecraft.

The door chime interrupted Picard's musing and Commander Riker entered from the bridge. "Captain, I think it would be useful to beam down for a close look at the *Onizuka*'s base camp."

Picard stood, his jaw tightening at Riker's suggestion. "Under the circumstances, I'd prefer not to lose any other crew members in Domaran limbo."

"And I'd prefer not getting lost," Riker said with a gallows grin. "But there may be some hints we just aren't picking up on long-range scans. I'd like Geordi with me—maybe he can see some other pieces to this puzzle."

Picard's expression made it clear he'd rather not authorize this away-team mission, if only he could think of an alternative entailing less risk. He couldn't. "All right, Number One. But make this visit as brief as possible."

If Will Riker had ever wanted to be anything but an explorer, he had long since forgotten those other dreams. Nothing had ever caught his fancy so much as the idea of going places no one had ever been, seeing wonders no one had ever witnessed before. Not that he'd been a thrillseeker or a daredevil. Quite the opposite, in fact. Even as a kid, when his friends had wanted to march boldly onto glaciers or dive headlong into unknown seas or descend into the damp darkness of caves, Will had usually been the one to make sure they were prepared and equipped for all eventualities.

The responsible one . . . the one who planned, and

packed their gear . . . the confident front man whom the others relied upon to assuage the trepidations of dubious parents eager to keep their sons and daughters home and unscathed, knowing all the while that these children needed to explore before they could grow up. *The responsible one.*

Of course, none of those childhood exploits had ever taken Will and his friends into the *real* unknown. The glaciers and caves and oceans of their adventures were, after all, usually in parks. But each autumn, fresh snows magically transformed the familiar Alaskan landscape that made up their backyard into wilderness as pristine as before the first human visitors had left their footprints in ancient snows, and that might have been enough to fire the imaginations of young boys and girls as they set out on their expeditions of discovery.

In time, though, they had all realized the truth. They had only been going where *they* had not gone before, as they followed the daring footsteps of generations of children before them. By the twenty-fourth century, there may have been a few dangerous places still left on Earth, but no unknown places. The real unknown, the infinite unknown, lay out in space.

For Riker, that path had been the only choice possible. And by now, years of experience had forced him to learn harsh lessons about the dark side of exploration. By definition, the unknown was also unpredictable. No matter how careful, how skilled, how prepared, no explorer could anticipate all eventualities. No mission was totally without dangers, and those dangers impossible to foresee were often the nastiest of all.

The field excursion to Domarus Four had seemed

about as close to risk-free as anything could be in this business. Riker hadn't had any special misgivings about sending the shuttle off on its own. But maybe he should have.

Maybe there was some warning sign I overlooked, he thought as he strode into the transporter room, with Geordi a step behind. *Maybe I should have known . . .*

Chief O'Brien stood behind the console as they mounted the steps to the transporter chamber. "Just the two of you, eh? Traveling light, I see," he quipped.

"Short trip," Riker said, without even a trace of his usual confident grin, though he did appreciate O'Brien's attempt to reduce the tension. It was one of the transporter chief's most valuable traits.

"I guess there won't be any time to ¬ick up some souvenirs for us, then?"

La Forge managed a gallows smile. "You never know. Maybe there'll be a convenient tourist trap."

"Energize," Riker said.

O'Brien activated the unit and two solid bodies began to shimmer.

On the bridge, Picard sank back into the firm contours of his command seat, thinking about the time he'd spent—wasted—trying to dig up nonexistent facts on the Tenirans. Normally, he'd simply have asked Data, and the android would have responded instantaneously. *Did I take Data for granted? He was so—*

Picard cut short the thought. *My God, I'm thinking of him in the past tense. I will not do that until—*

"Captain," Worf said sharply. "Those energy patterns—"

On the main viewscreen, Picard and the rest of the

bridge staff saw colorful tendrils dancing and darting outside the *Enterprise,* and around the Teniran vessel, too.

Two shafts of sparkling transporter energy touched the grassy ground of Domarus Four. As they solidified into Riker and La Forge, they were wrapped in a cloud of shifting colors. At the moment they completed transport, the mystified officers heard a vague and distant sound, like dissonant chimes. An instant later, the sounds and colors faded quickly away.

Picard stood close to the large viewscreen, staring out in a mixture of wonder and concern as the swirls of energy pinwheeled around the *Enterprise*—though apparently causing no damage, and barely registering on sensors.

"What the devil," Picard muttered. "Lieutenant Worf, report."

"It is the identical energy pattern as before, Captain, surrounding the ship—both ships."

Before Worf could continue, the shifting veil of colors burst into a spray of glittering particles and faded as suddenly as they'd appeared. Picard was on his feet, facing his security chief.

"Lieutenant, if that was energy, why didn't our shields activate automatically?"

"I do not know, sir. I will run a diagnostic scan of shield and sensor systems immediately." Worf paused. "Message from the away team, sir."

"On audio."

"Captain," Riker's voice said over the speaker, "we just saw the damndest thing."

Picard listened to Riker's report, intrigued by the coincident similarities. "As you were beaming down,

Number One, we saw those same energy patterns out in space, around both ships."

"And then they just disappeared?"

"Just like some sort of cosmic Cheshire cat."

"Hmm. I don't think I like the sound of that, Captain," Riker said, a telltale grimness in his voice. "We'll make our visit to Wonderland as brief as possible. Riker out."

"Captain," said Worf, "the Tenirans are hailing us."

Picard remained standing. Sometimes he simply felt more authoritative that way. "On screen, Lieutenant."

Once again, the unsmiling face of Captain Arit replaced Domarus Four on the main viewer. "Picard, we know that you have beamed people down to our world without permission, and we warned you that—"

"This debate is getting tiresome, Captain Arit. We do not acknowledge the validity of your claim."

"This hostile act will not be tolerated."

"Our away team is not hostile, Captain," Picard said forcefully, centering himself under the bridge's transparent dome. "We are searching for clues to the whereabouts of our shuttlecraft—"

"Which disappeared from space, not the planet. You have no right to—"

"We have *every* right to pursue all possibilities that may present themselves in our search . . ."

"Not on *our* planet," Arit shot back.

She continued her lecture, but Picard's attention drifted from the viewscreen as he felt a sudden tingling sensation, like prickly feathers brushing against bare skin. Then he saw a tentative curl of color appear inside the bridge, just fluttering in mid-air as if trying to decide what to do next. As before, it didn't remain a single color long enough to be labeled as red or blue or any other definite shade. As it changed continuously, it also grew, spiraling slowly around the circumference of the bridge.

". . . and a Teniran security squad will beam down and take custody of your away team," Arit went on, though Picard was barely listening now.

As the multicolored whorls wafted about him, he heard the same random tinkling Riker had described encountering on the planet. "Worf, internal sensor scan," he murmured. Then he deftly replied to Arit's threats without missing a beat—fully aware that as he spoke, the intensity of the sounds and colors increased. "Do not challenge the *Enterprise,* Captain. Domarus may not be uninhabited, and we will not permit the taking of hostages in your attempt to—"

"What is that? Jevlin—what—what *is* it?" Arit said, her own attention now clearly distracted from her sparring with Picard. *"Enterprise,* if this is an attack—"

"I assure you—we are not attacking your ship."

Without warning, the colorful swirls deepened, thickened and blew into a vortex around Picard.

Worf's eyes grew wide. *"Captain!"* Paying no heed to Arit's frantic threat of retaliation coming through the comm speaker, Worf vaulted the railing, his muscular body stretched out in a headlong dive, hoping to wrench Picard free of the inexplicable force surrounding him. But before the security chief could reach him, the vortex and Picard disappeared in a scintillating haze.

With a grunt, Worf landed hard on the deck, rolled quickly and saw that he'd failed. He felt a bellow of frustrated rage welling up from his gut—and forced it back just as he realized that *he* was now in command.

Chapter Four

WORF SCRAMBLED to his feet, trying to control the torrent of anger and shame he felt rushing through him like a storm-driven tide.

"Enterprise! Enterprise! What have you done with Captain Arit?"

As he heard this new and panicky voice squawking from the comm speaker, Worf willed himself to concentrate and take its measure—*male, but not at all commanding . . . filled with fear.*

As security chief, his instincts as a natural warrior could be permitted freer reign. But if he'd learned anything from his time in Starfleet, the role of successful commander required more nuance, the sort of thing that went against his hereditary impulses. But nothing he couldn't handle.

"Enterprise," the voice repeated, with no less breathless hysteria, "what have you done with—"

"This is the *Enterprise,"* the big Klingon said as he settled into the captain's empty seat, his voice low and deliberate. "Identify yourself."

"Jevlin, first officer of the *Glin-Kale*—my captain was talking with Picard—just talking. Then those colors—they—they filled our bridge—and then she was *gone*. What did you do?"

"Interesting. But we have done nothing with your captain. *Enterprise* out." Then, maintaining his calm demeanor, Worf called the away team. "Commander Riker, the captain . . . has vanished, just like the shuttlecraft."

"Dammit. Beam us up *now,* Worf."

In all the years since he'd given up the fiery pleasures of *peroheen* wine, there'd been more than a few times when Jevlin had found his resolve weakening. On more than a few occasions, he'd been so tempted to seek solace in a bottle that he could feel that old familiar burning down his throat despite being nowhere near a drink.

But he'd never felt that way more than now. And he found himself in Arit's cabin—*good thing she didn't let me fix that door or I might not've been able to get in*—holding the same bottle she'd been holding earlier. He noticed it was considerably closer to empty than the last time he'd seen it, and that hadn't been so long ago. *Whatever else they say about the cap'n, she sure could hold her wine.*

The sound of footsteps in the doorway startled him and he nearly dropped the bottle.

"I want my mother to come back, Jevlin," said a small, composed voice.

Jevlin didn't move, and he squeezed his eyes closed. He didn't want to face Captain Arit's little girl. Then he felt a hand resting firmly on his shoulder.

"You miss her, too, don't you," said Keela.

With a sigh, the grizzled old officer put the bottle

down and turned to face the six-year-old. "Yes, Keela, I do." He rubbed his own rheumy eyes as he noticed that hers were clear and wide.

"Have you been crying?" she asked. She formed her words with the precocious precision of a child more accustomed to conversation with adults than with her peers.

"No," he said, more gruffly than he'd intended. "Well . . . almost . . . maybe a little. Have you?"

Her lower lip quivered for a moment, revealing one tiny juvenile fang. The one on the other side had fallen out recently. "No . . . mother wouldn't want me to." She pointed at the bottle. "Is that juice? Can I have some?"

Jevlin coughed out a short chuckle. "Uhh—no, it's not juice. How do you know your mother wouldn't want you to cry?"

"Because I'm the captain's daughter. I have to be strong like her. And she's told me she might die someday, like father did on Ziakk Five. We all might. It's just the way things are."

"They are, are they?"

Keela nodded, the downy forelock of her mane falling across her brow. She brushed it away. "That's right. Mother said it's nothing to be sad about. She said we've lived a hard life and dying might be better."

"Oh, she did, did she?" Jevlin huffed, making no attempt to hide his annoyance. "Well, your mother's too much of a fatalist, if you ask me."

The little girl cocked her head. "What's a fatalist?"

"That's someone who believes the worst will happen, no matter what."

Keela shoved her way into his lap. "Do you think mother is dead?"

The direct innocence of the question sliced through

to Jevlin's heart. He felt his eyes misting and he struggled to retain control. "Uhh—that's some question, Keela. I—uhh—I'm not sure."

"Are you a fatalist then?"

He looked into Keela's preternaturally solemn eyes. "No, no, I'm not," he said softly. "And I do think your mother is alive."

Keela smiled. "So do I. And I know that's not juice . . . and I won't tell her you drank some."

"Quick thinking, Mr. Worf—and commendable discretion," Riker said as he took a seat at one end of the long curved table in the conference lounge.

"I saw no need for the Tenirans to know that Captain Picard had also been taken," Worf said.

Dr. Crusher raised an eyebrow. "Taken. So we're going on the belief that our shuttle and both captains were . . . *transported* . . . intentionally?"

"Until and unless a better hypothesis comes along, yes," Riker said. "Do you disagree, Doctor?"

"No—but we still don't have answers to a lot of key questions."

Engineer La Forge nodded in agreement. "Like who or what grabbed them—not to mention, why, where and how."

Riker scanned the faces of the others. "Anybody have any ideas?"

"I'd bet a week's pay they're all on Domarus somewhere," Geordi said.

"Based on what?" Riker asked, his skepticism revealed by the creases on his forehead.

"Well, for one thing, we don't have any reason to think they're anyplace else."

"I'll agree that's a reasonable starting point," Riker said. "Go on."

"Even though we haven't been able to pin down a specific source for those energy patterns," Geordi said, "I think it's better than even money they're originating on the planet somewhere."

"Some*how*, some*where*," Riker said sourly. As much as the fate of the missing shuttle and crew concerned him, Riker had always regarded the safety of the captain as his special trust. Picard's disappearance raised the situation to a whole new level of urgency. "Those aren't my favorite words. We need specifics and we need them fast."

Standing astride the crest of a grassy knoll, Jean-Luc Picard squinted into the afternoon sun hanging high in the soft blue sky of Domarus Four. At least, he *assumed* it was Domarus Four beneath his feet. Whatever force had whisked him off the bridge, he hoped it hadn't had the power to sweep him any farther off than the planet around which the *Enterprise* had been orbiting.

I hope she's still up there . . .

As abductions went, this was proving to be an odd one. Without warning or threat, he'd been removed from his bridge and deposited here . . . wherever he was. But there wasn't a soul to greet, berate or imprison him. It seemed he was free to wander.

But wander where? He'd strolled through woods and fields for the better part of an hour, observing, wondering why he was here, wondering if his crew had any idea of his whereabouts. He tapped his chest communicator.

"Picard to *Enterprise*. Picard to *Enterprise*—do you read me?" After only an obligatory couple of seconds, he muttered, "Still not working." He had no reason to believe the device would suddenly resume function when it apparently hadn't worked from the moment he'd materialized here. As soon as he'd made that dismaying but not unexpected discovery, he'd proceeded on the assumption that the communicator's bio-telemetry signal normally monitored and tracked by ship's sensors was also inoperative, or blocked from reception by the starship orbiting fifty-thousand kilometers out in space.

If he was indeed alone and stranded, Picard decided quickly that he'd better see about survival needs. The daytime climate was pleasant, not unlike a warm spring day back home in Labarre, in the heart of French wine country—soothing sun, fresh breeze— just the sort of day his family might have left the Picard vineyards for a picnic on the bank of the river that meandered past the village. Though he couldn't be certain, he doubted such a mild day would turn dangerously cold at night, so exposure to the elements probably posed no immediate threat.

Plants grew in abundance here, and he expected he'd be able to find some edible vegetation without being poisoned. This much plant life indicated generous rainfall, and Picard hoped he'd find some open source of water in the vicinity. A pond or stream would fill his needs nicely.

Between the walkabout and the warm sun, he'd become quite thirsty—he'd need to find potable water sooner or later, so now seemed as good a time as any. As he paused on the knoll, the knee-high grass around him bowing in the breeze, Picard caught the sound of rushing water nearby.

It didn't take him long to find it—a fast-flowing stream three meters across, perhaps a meter deep, and clear enough to see the bottom. He crouched on the bank, his boots compacting the gravelly sand beneath his feet as he dipped his hands in and let the icy water run through his fingers. Then he cupped them and scooped the water to his mouth, gulping it down. *Thirstier than I realized . . .*

He bent forward for another serving, and noticed some fish at least as long as his forearm swimming lazily past him.

A bit full of themselves, he thought. *Presumably the top of the food chain in these parts. Well, that may change if I get hungry enough . . .*

Picard shook his hands in the warm air and dried them on his pants, then touched his communicator. "Personal log, continued. Starvation does not seem to be a concern here. In addition to the flora already mentioned, I have located a fresh-water stream with plenty of fish . . ."

He glanced at a sizable specimen which seemed to be bucking the current just to stare out at this odd creature encroaching on its wet domain. ". . . Though I am as yet uncertain of how to catch these fish. The challenge may be a welcome diversion. I've been on this planet for nearly one hour, and still have no hint of who or what transported me here—or why. Yet . . . I do not feel in any danger. And, though I can't explain the feeling, I believe my presence here *will* help solve the riddles of this place."

Deanna Troi was no stranger to darkness, which was after all a major environmental component of a life spent traveling through the void of deep space. But even in space, darkness was rarely absolute. There were always the stars.

For the past two hours, though, Troi and her companions had been trapped in the shuttlecraft, in some place as dark as any she'd ever experienced.

How they got here—wherever here *was*—they had no idea. With no exterior lights working, all they could see through the windows was virtual blackness, as if the craft had been sealed inside a box. Without operative sensors, they had no notion of what might be outside, so she and Data opted to postpone any exploratory ventures either until they had scanners running again—or until repair work proved totally futile, at which point they would reassess the risks of reconnaissance.

As Data organized a strategy aimed at most efficiently resuscitating the shuttle's inert systems, the Betazoid counselor concentrated on monitoring the psychological equilibrium of her three teen-aged charges. Their feelings and undercurrents had run the expected range, from intense initial fear to a more considered evaluation of their circumstances once the heart-pounding threat of imminent destruction had evaporated.

Now, the two boys were crammed into the cockpit, under Data's supervision, while Gina had been assigned to the rerouting of back-up sensor circuitry, a job that required her to kneel in order to gain comfortable access to the innards of the rear-cabin console. After fifteen hunched-over minutes of determined work on delicate electronic components, Gina slumped and lay on her back, stretching her kinked muscles by the glow of a single lantern.

"Counselor Troi, are you bored?"

"Are you?"

"Is a sun hot?" Gina answered dully as she sat up, hugging her knees to her chest. "You bet I'm bored. It feels like we've been here for *weeks,* not hours."

"What else do you feel?"

"Hmm." Gina's face scrunched thoughtfully. "If I

56

don't get out of this teeny-tiny shuttle soon, I might just go stark-raving bonkers—?"

"I see," Troi said with patient amusement.

Gina picked up the lack of urgent concern in Troi's voice. "I guess you don't think I'm about to crack under the pressure?"

"I don't think so, Gina. The feelings you're having are entirely normal for anyone in this situation, especially adolescents. In fact, if you *didn't* have them, *then* I'd be worried."

"Hyper-hormones, huh?"

Troi let a laugh slip out. "Something like that. Adolescents are still struggling with the childish impulse for instant gratification. You three are much brighter and more mature than many of your peers, so you're much better equipped to deal with those feelings."

"Are you sure about that?" Gina asked, her brows rising into a dubious arch.

"You verbalized your feelings rather than acting on them. That's a sign of maturity and—"

Deanna stopped short when half the consoles and cabin lights flickered back to life.

"Yippeee!" Gina clapped her hands as she whooped, then looked mortified. "That wasn't a sign of maturity, was it?"

"Mmm . . . it'll be our little secret." Troi's part of the secret was that she'd felt like cheering, too.

They both looked up as Data appeared at the mid-ship opening leading to the cockpit, a central spot from which he could address all hands. "Gina, Wesley and Ken—you have all been most helpful," the android said as Troi gave him an approving nod. "Main life-support systems and scanner arrays are now restored to stable and fully operative status."

Gina raised a tentative hand. "Should I activate exterior illumination, Commander?"

"Affirmative, Gina. I believe it is time we got a comprehensive look at our immediate surroundings."

As the others pressed their faces to the nearest windows, Gina clambered to her feet, slid into the chair at her console and keyed three of the shuttle's running lights and spots for wide-beam. As the lights flashed on, they revealed that the shuttle had somehow been deposited inside a cavern, high-domed, but little more than ten or fifteen meters across—and for just a fleeting moment, the compact vessel was surrounded by a multi-colored swirl, the same as they'd seen in space. But the ribbons of color reacted as if they'd been frightened by the sudden brightness of the shuttle's lights and they vanished in an instant, quickly enough to make Troi wonder if they'd truly been there.

As the apparent reality of where they were trapped took root, Troi herself felt what she could tell the younger crew members were feeling—dismay, coupled with as yet unanswerable questions. Gina was the first to voice that common reaction.

"Where in god's name are we?" She peered out the viewport, craning her head from side to side, trying to take in all the eerie beauty of the cavern, with glittering mineral deposits studding its walls and rocky arches—yet hoping to see something other than what was there.

"It would appear," said Data, looking over her shoulder, "that we are in a cavern."

"But a cavern *where,* Data," Troi wondered. "Are we inside Domarus Four? And if we are, how did we get here?"

"There is no way to be certain. But until and unless

58

we uncover evidence to the contrary, the most likely conclusion is that we are indeed inside Domarus Four. As to how we got here, I believe the phrase is 'Your guess is as good as mine.'"

Wesley poked his head back from the cockpit. "Commander, now that we've got sensors working, should we run a scan and find out what's out there?"

"Please do so, Ensign, with Ken's assistance. We will need to know the atmospheric composition of our immediate environment—particularly whether it poses any immediate risk to us and the shuttlecraft. Gina, I would like you to pay specific attention to spectro-analysis of the cave's geological makeup and structure."

As the young away-team members busied themselves, Troi leaned close to Data and spoke confidentially. "I'm concerned about them."

"How so, Counselor?"

"When those lights came on, I felt fear in all of them, even Wesley."

Data nodded. "Is that not natural?"

"Oh, yes. And though they are too well-trained to be paralyzed by fear, it is not going to disappear. The longer we're here, the more they are going to look to us to help them deal with that fear."

"Ahh." Data paused for a moment's consideration of Troi's prediction. "And what should we do to deal with that?"

"Actually, what you're doing is fine."

"Oh. That is encouraging." Data's eyes brightened with pleasure at the notion that he had provided appropriate support for fragile human psyches. But then his brow furrowed as if he'd run across a previously overlooked gap in his programming. "And . . . what is it that I am doing?"

Troi smiled reassuringly. Data was the most guile-less being she'd ever known, a characteristic she still found as charming as the day they'd first met. "Keeping them occupied—treating them as important members of this crew."

"I see. Then that will be an easy strategy to continue, Counselor . . . they *are* important members of this crew."

Chapter Five

Gone Fishing . . .

I'd put up a sign, Picard thought as he hiked back toward the stream, *but who's to care* where *I've gone?*

By the position of the Domaran sun, he guessed it to be mid-afternoon. He'd done a bit more scouting of his immediate vicinity and judged it a nice enough setting for a vacation cottage, though he'd have preferred some more choice in the matter than had been offered by the manner in which he'd been whisked off the *Enterprise* without word or warning.

With no way to figure the eventual duration of his stay here, he'd also picked out a suitable spot for an overnight camp—a crested clearing bounded by woods on two sides and hills on the other two. In addition to being relatively high ground, the campsite offered proximity to a ready supply of firewood—though he didn't have any tree-chopping tools, he'd seen plenty of branches lying on the ground during an exploratory stroll through the woods. There were also some small caves nicked into the nearby rocky hill-sides, apparently uninhabited by any native animal life, and more than adequate in case he needed a more protected place to stay.

Next concern—how to catch dinner. He'd considered—briefly—the most basic fishing method: bare hands. But Picard recognized the reality that he wasn't quite that elemental, and he had a hard time picturing himself swiping at leaping fish like some wild bear. With no sporting goods shops in sight, and nothing likely to be serviceable as fishing line to attach to a rod, he decided on a reasonable compromise—spearfishing. He'd never attempted it himself, but he'd seen the age-old technique demonstrated by practitioners from various human and alien cultures. The principle was straightforward enough. It remained to be seen how that would translate into practice.

He sat on the stream bank, near the water and next to a batch of straight, slender branches, all at least a meter long, collected in the woods to be made into spears. Using a rough stone he'd found, he whittled and filed the ends of the best branches into lethal points. As he worked, he heard occasional splashes of fish breaking the stream's surface.

Are they exercising or doing reconnaissance? he wondered as he watched their acrobatics. Picard couldn't help smiling as he remembered how indifferent a fisherman he'd been as a boy. He'd tag along with his brother Robert when he and the other older boys in their village would go to fish in the river or the lake near the family vineyards. Robert had usually considered little Jean-Luc's presence an embarrassment, but their mother would strongly suggest that he take his younger brother along . . . *though I'm not sure why I wanted to go.*

Picard paused to examine his craftsmanship. Two other spears were done, but this one wasn't quite ready. With smooth strokes, he grated stone against wood, sending fine chips and dust flying. *Perhaps I just didn't want to be left out.* He chuckled at a rueful memory—Robert mocking him mercilessly because of his distaste for grasping wriggling worms with his fingers and impaling them on sharp hooks—*the worms, not my fingers*—*though a fair number of fingertips were pierced in the process.*

Finally satisfied with his third spear, Picard set it down with the others and leaned forward, watching the fish darting about in the clear stream, recalling later trips to the lake without sibling supervision. No longer compelled by peer pressure to fish, he'd learned the joys of just rowing out with a few friends for conversation and contemplation, luxuriating in the tranquil warmth of the sun and the soothing lap of the water against the boat. *Ahh . . . and there was no more ideal setting in which to woo a young lady in romantic privacy . . . as long as obnoxious friends didn't seek you out with the express intention of starting a splash fight.*

Picard stood up and hefted the different spears, checking for feel and balance. With a shrug, he decided none of them exactly constituted a finely tooled weapon and simply chose one at random; he tossed the other two onto the pile of unfinished branches where they landed with a clatter.

If this works, Picard thought as he reached the water's edge, *perhaps I might try my hand at penning a novel—The Old Captain and the Stream.*

He drew his arm back, waited with the spear head high for an unsuspecting fish to swim within range, then hurled it—

—and watched the fish dart away as the spear point split the stream's surface and drove itself into the muddy bottom, stirring up enough silt to thoroughly cloud the formerly clear water. Perhaps this wasn't going to be as easy as he'd hoped.

He bent down, snatched up another spear and set himself once again. A pair of fish drifted close and his arm snapped forward. The spear cut through the water and missed again.

Third try—arm cocked—and a third failure. And all three spears were now embedded in the mud, the ends of their shafts sticking up out of the water. Out of Picard's dry-land reach. He had a choice: make new ones or retrieve the old.

It was obviously more efficient to get the existing spears. He didn't want to get his boots wet and didn't feel like taking them off, so he mapped out a cautious approach to the weapons. All he had to do was step carefully on a few rocks rising partway above the stream's surface.

"Not very good at this, are you, Picard?"

The totally unexpected sound of a voice startled him, but he located the source immediately—the other side of the stream, the edge of the forest, about thirty meters back from the far bank.

"Captain Arit, I presume?" he called across. "So—we were both brought here. Interesting."

"No one said I was brought here."

"Came on your own, then, did you?" His tone, dry and skeptical, made it clear he didn't believe that for an instant. "How long have you been watching?"

The Teniran commander moved a couple of wary strides toward the water, then stopped as if she preferred not to stray from the sanctuary of the forest behind her.

"Your whole sorry attempt."

"Can you do better?" he challenged amiably as he stood on the shore with his hands on his hips.

"Probably."

Picard sensed a careful confidence in her reply. "Care to try?"

"No."

"We'll need food."

"It could be a long time coming at the rate you're going, Picard."

"How long have you been here on the planet?" He waited for an answer that obviously wasn't coming. What was Captain Arit's secret? Hoping to elicit a tad more trust, he answered his own question. "I'd say I arrived about three hours ago. I haven't been able to establish contact with my ship. I'm assuming the facts are very much the same in your case—?"

"Assume all you want, Picard," Arit said, then turned and disappeared into the trees.

Picard watched her go, then shrugged to himself. "Strange."

Back to fishing. Or, to be more accurate, back to spear retrieval. He took a measured step out onto the closest rock, making sure it was firmly placed in the stream bed. It seemed solid enough. Two more short strides and he'd be able to reach the spears.

Perhaps Arit was right about his not being especially proficient at all this. Then again, he'd had no right or reason to expect instant success. Who would? Still, he had faith in his coordination and believed he'd get the gist of it soon enough. He stepped onto the next flat stone with his other foot—and slipped on a fine coating of damp moss. He teetered for a short eternity, failed to regain his footing and toppled sideways into the water.

From somewhere on the fringe of the forest, he heard the distinctly annoying sound of laughter.

The hatch to the *Glin-Kale*'s bridge slid halfway open, groaned, creaked and jammed. Jevlin glared at the wall panel housing the mechanism, then whacked it with his walking stick. The door opened the rest of the way.

He entered—then, much like the hesitant hatch, halted in mid-hobble when he saw Valend Egin waiting for him. "Is there some incredibly good reason for you to be on the bridge, Egin?"

"I'll thank you to address me by my rightful title, Jevlin."

"Yes, I'm sure you would. So I'll save us both the trouble," the old first officer muttered as he moved to the operations console just left of the empty command chair.

"I have every right to be on the bridge."

"I suppose you do. Just don't get in our way . . . *Valend.*" Jevlin turned to the female officer seated at the console. She was hardly more than a child, her mane still short and downy, not the luxuriant fur of a mature Teniran adult. *How qualified can she be? How much experience can she have? Are we that desperate that we put children to work on the bridge?*

He knew the answer to that: *Yes.* Vital posts had to be attended, and the critical losses suffered in the Ziakk Five disaster left few choices. Anyone who could do a job did it, regardless of age.

"I—I'm sorry, sir," she said, sitting stiffly in her seat. "I haven't been able to locate Captain Arit down on the planet. Sensors just don't seem to be working right. I—I'll keep trying, sir—that is, if you want me to."

Jevlin gave her an avuncular wink. "That's the spirit, Mahdolin. Can't imagine where else the cap'n might be. Just keep up the good work." He turned toward the command chair, and found Egin blocking his way.

"Jevlin, how long do we look for her?"

"You sound like you're ready to quit."

"The reality is, she may be gone. We may *never*—"

"She's *not* gone," Jevlin shot back, his tone more charged than he'd intended. He sensed the half-dozen crewmen working about the bridge glancing his way and damned himself for giving Egin the satisfaction of so much attention. But Egin had this knack for taxing anyone's patience to the breaking point. *As long as I can keep from pounding him with this old walking stick . . .* "What would you have us do?"

"Start colonizing this planet *now,* before the Federation ship can stop us."

Jevlin just stared, then spoke through gritted teeth. "You . . . are . . ." He took a deep breath, tightened his grip on his stick, then lowered his voice to a ragged whisper. "That . . . is not wise . . . not until we know what's happened to Arit . . . and surely not until we have a pretty good idea it's safe down there."

"I want—"

"Jevlin, I don't *care* what you want. With Cap'n Arit off the ship, *I'm* in command. And I'll not risk another precious Teniran life without good cause just because you want to start your make-believe government. Now, I've got work to do, so if you'll excuse me."

With that, Jevlin turned his back on the sputtering Egin and stalked off the bridge, thankful that *this* time the balky hatch shut behind him.

He made his way down toward the engineering deck, wishing there were some alternate route—one where he wouldn't have to pass shabbily clothed families with their meager salvaged belongings, closely huddled in crowded corridors. Huddled for warmth in the underheated lower-level passageways. Huddled because space was at a premium. Huddled because the ones who had come this far needed to feel the touch of those who had survived with them.

Though Jevlin knew it would be easier on him to avoid looking into their faces as he limped by, he couldn't help it. They weren't cargo, and he couldn't bear to treat them that way. Meeting their gazes might somehow make these refugees believe that they mattered. It wasn't much, but it was all he could do for them for now.

Arriving at the engineering compartment, he found that the entry door had been wedged three-quarters open by technicians weary of wondering whether or not it would operate, and Jevlin eased through. He found a rail-thin officer, as old and grizzled as himself, leaning over a workbench with electronic components and diagnostic tools spread haphazardly across its surface. To Jevlin's untutored eye, it looked like some old computerized gadget had blown apart under extreme stress. Then again, sometimes it seemed like their whole ship was only a short step away from suffering a similar fate. "Chief."

The engineer glanced up from his repair work. "It took you long enough to get here."

Jevlin's brows arched. "Don't move as fast as I used to—and neither do you, Naladi."

"And neither does the old *Glin-Kale,* I'm afraid."

"She's still here . . . how bad can it be?"

Naladi prefaced his words with a sigh. "Bad enough."

Jevlin waved at the parts scattered atop the workbench. "This stuff?"

"This? This is my relaxation break, trying to see if I can salvage anything for us to use later. Take a look, Jevlin." The chief engineer swiveled to face his adjacent desk, and reached over to key his computer board as Jevlin leaned over for a closer look. A diagnostic schematic appeared on a screen mottled with dust and streaked by fingertips that had made a halfhearted attempt to wipe it clean. This place was just as disordered and unkempt as the rest of the ship, an observation that Jevlin found distressing. It even smelled stale. Chief Naladi used to be obsessed with having everything spit-shined and spotless. Nowadays, it was all he could do to keep the *Glin-Kale* running.

"She may not be running for long," Naladi said, as if reading the first officer's mind. "The reactor chamber fields are getting fuzzy around the edges. If they don't hold—"

"I know, I know. Can you do anything?"

"You know me. We're already doing it. We'll manage."

"I do know you, Naladi," Jevlin said with a grin. "You're always whining about the end being near—and it never is."

"Not yet anyway. Leaving so soon? You've been no fun at all since you divorced the bottle."

"I've got an important appointment. Keep me posted."

The engineer gave him a dismissive wave. "Yeah, sure, sure, limp off and leave me with my problems. What do you care."

"You shouldn't have done all this yourself," Jevlin scolded, waggling his finger at little Keela.

She perched kneeling on a chair at the small oblong table in her family quarters, upon which she'd arranged place-settings for two—tarnished utensils, chipped mugs and the one pristine piece on the table, an elegant ceramic urn with steam rising from its long spout. A platter filled with a dozen small, neatly arranged finger biscuits sat in the center of the table.

"But I *always* do it myself. Mother doesn't have time. She says if I want to have tea with her every afternoon, I'm the one who has to make it. Now sit down," she said, her tiny hand pointing impatiently at the opposite chair.

Jevlin joined her at the table. "Didn't your mother worry—I mean, *doesn't* she worry about you burning yourself?"

"Really, Jevlin," Keela said with a roll of her eyes, "only *children* burn themselves."

"Ahh. Of course. How foolish of me." He reached for the urn.

"No," she squawked.

He yanked his hand back as if *he'd* been burned. "I was just going to pour it, Keela."

"We have to say our quiet thank-yous and hopes first, silly. Mother taught me that was why tea time was invented."

"And your mother was absolutely right, Keela. So let's close our eyes and look to the stars." He watched as the little girl tipped her head back and her eyelids fluttered shut. He knew she'd be imagining a perfect night sky, just as he'd done when he was a child, just as all Teniran children were taught to do—imagining the deepest black, strewn with the glitter of starlight. Her lips moved just slightly as she silently whispered her own list. Then her eyes opened.

"Did you peek, Jevlin?"

He stiffened in mock indignity. "I would *never* do that. Might keep your hopes from coming true. I do know that much. I may be old, but I still remember things, Keela."

"Just checking. You can pour the tea now."

"Thank you, your ladyship." He tipped the urn and filled her cup first, then watched as she held it in both her hands and sniffed the sweet-scented steam curling up toward her face. Pouring his own cupful, he handed her a biscuit and took one for himself.

"Thank you, Jevlin."

"You're welcome. And thank you for inviting me. I hope your mother is having her own tea time now, wherever she is."

"Me too," Keela said with a solemn nod. "She gets very grumpy if she doesn't."

Beverly Crusher sat alone in Ten-Forward, tucked in a corner booth facing the big observation windows, as far off the natural path of traffic as possible. She really didn't want company, but she did want a snack. And she also wanted a change of scenery from sickbay and her quarters. So she risked the inevitable—friends and crewmates certain to approach her with well-meaning sympathy and encouragement.

Guinan was the first. Of course, greeting and serving patrons of the starship's lounge was her job, so her arrival in Beverly's corner was more or less expected. Once she brought over Bev's apple pie à la mode and the accompanying cup of herbal tea, perhaps she'd take the nonverbal hint and move off to more chatty clientele. Beverly fervently hoped so.

But Guinan didn't go. Business was slow, and she sat. "How are you doing?"

Crusher managed a wan fraction of a smile. "Fine."

She dug up a forkful of pie and got mostly dry crust. But she felt Guinan's inscrutable gaze on her. Not staring—no, Guinan was a being of impeccable manners and never stared the way humans might. It was just a gentle, never-wavering look that wordlessly invited its subject to loosen up, and speak up. And it usually worked. But this time, Beverly fought it.

"Look," Guinan finally said, "I'm the last one to pry. And I know you and Counselor Troi are like this . . ." She raised her hand with two fingers held tightly side-by-side. ". . . but I'm here if you just feel like talking."

"Thanks, Guinan. But right now, I just feel like eating."

Guinan stood. "Say no more." She backed away, pointing a thumb toward the bar across the room. "I'm right over there."

Cloaked again in her preferred solitude, Dr. Crusher nibbled on her pie. Guinan was right. Deanna *would* be the first one she'd go to if she wanted to air her fears about Wesley's safety. But Deanna was missing, too—and Beverly was worried about her friend as well as her son.

Then there was Jean-Luc. Her relationship with the captain was considerably more complicated than her friendship with Troi. Troi was like a sister and best buddy all rolled into one, as close to her now as the best friends with whom she'd shared slumber parties and college dorm rooms when she was growing up.

Not that Jean-Luc wasn't also her friend. But there was more. She'd long since absolved Picard of any responsibility for her husband's death. Long since sorted out nasty feelings of ambivalence, which had understandably grown from the circumstances of Jack's death while under Picard's command. Once she got her assignment to the *Enterprise,* it would have been impossible for her to not have had mixed feelings about serving with the captain who'd brought her husband's body home.

But that was then. Now, it was a question of how she and Jean-Luc really felt about each other. Here. Today. Perhaps they'd never be certain. Lord knows, they'd tiptoed around it on enough occasions. Perhaps the requirements of their professional responsibilities precluded any relationship other than friendship. Never mind the emotional baggage related to their past—the truth was, she wouldn't hesitate to come to Picard if she needed a supportive word.

But *dammit*—*he* was missing too. And maybe she

didn't want to talk to anyone about Wesley's being lost out there, on this unknown planet—

"Looks good," said a warm masculine voice, interrupting her musings. "The pie, I mean. Mind if I join you?"

Beverly found herself looking up at Will Riker, his eyes crinkling as he smiled. Her expression remained blank for the long moment it took her to shift her brain back into a conversation mode. "Actually—"

"Yes?"

"Don't take this personally, Will, but I'd rather be by myself."

"Oh." Riker looked crestfallen. "Well. Umm . . . I just thought you might want somebody to talk to about—"

"I don't. Really. I'm fine. Thanks."

Nodding as he retreated, but looking thoroughly unconvinced, Riker headed for the bar.

And Dr. Crusher stared out the windows—past the planet, toward the distant stars—and whittled away at her ice cream and pie.

Until she felt another presence behind her. *Oh, Lord . . . not again . . .*

"Hi, Geordi," she said, trying to sound mildly appreciative but not too inviting.

"Hi, Doc. Checking out the planet?"

"Actually, no. I was looking at the stars."

Geordi's brow wrinkled above his VISOR as her answer caught him off-guard. "Oh. I figured because of Wes . . . Uhh . . . y'know, what with the shuttle and all . . ." He licked his lips. "Uhh, he's a good kid, Doc . . . he'll be okay. He's with Data, and Data always comes back."

74

"Thanks, Geordi. Really. Thanks. But I just kind of wanted to be by myself." The chief engineer seemed to take the gentle brush-off with great relief and he too headed for the bar.

Beverly smiled to herself as she washed down a bite of pie with a sip of tea. *They're all so sweet to care about how I feel . . . but I just don't want to talk about it. How can I explain that? And why should I have to explain it?* She felt the worries welling up again, the ones she'd hoped she'd swallowed with the ice cream and pie.

And, again, she sensed someone over her shoulder. She turned slightly to see the looming bulk of Lieutenant Worf. She sighed out loud, wondering if all one-thousand people living aboard the *Enterprise* were going to pay sympathy calls.

Worf sidled around the table so he could face her. "Doctor, I—"

Suddenly, her emotional dam broke and the flood of fears rushed out of her. Though she spoke softly, the words came so fast that she almost didn't know what she was saying. And at the same time, she knew every syllable before it passed her lips. They spelled out all the cares and concerns of a lifetime of motherhood, all crystallized by the inescapable reality *right now* that she might have to deal with the death of her son.

They were right on target, all of her friends—Guinan and Will and Geordi. She *did* need to talk, to share her mortal dreads with someone. And then, just as abruptly as the torrent of feelings and fears had begun, it stopped. And one shocked thought roamed around inside her head: *Why did I dump this on Worf, of all people?!*

As she caught her breath, she looked up at him standing stiffly, looking like he wanted to be somewhere else, anywhere else—and she suddenly knew why. Like Crusher, and unlike those other good friends, Worf had a son. Little Alexander, Worf's child with Ambassador K'eylahr—a secret K'eylahr had only recently revealed to him, just before her murder by a Klingon traitor.

Worf had probably been the last person Crusher expected to harbor even a shred of parental instinct. But it had come to him as it came to any human parent—mystically, instantly. *Love* . . . And it had led him, without a second thought, to exalt his young son's best interests above his own.

Worf had sent the child to live on Earth, with his own human foster parents. And though the *Enterprise*'s Klingon warrior never spoke of his feelings, Beverly somehow knew from that one selfless act that Worf knew exactly how she felt at this moment.

"I'm sorry, Worf," she said with an embarrassed smile. "I didn't mean to hit you with all that."

Unable to look her quite in the eye, he took a measured breath and spoke like a man afraid to crack the very thin ice on which he stood. "I . . . I came to ask you if I could postpone my scheduled physical until next week."

Beverly felt herself blush. "Oh," she said in a tiny, mortified voice. She felt as if she'd been glimpsed naked. But there was no cover-up close at hand. "Yes, uhh . . . of course . . . that would be fine . . . no problem at all."

Then she looked away. And Worf scuttled out of Ten-Forward.

* * *

Though he was due back on duty in a little while, and had in fact been headed back to the bridge to begin his shift early, Worf left the ship's lounge and detoured back to his cabin. He sat at his communications console.

"Computer . . . I would like to record a star-mail message . . . to be sent to Earth. To Sergey and Helena Rozhenko . . . and Alexander. Address on file." Worf took a deep breath and set himself in front of the recorder. "Hello, Mother and Father . . . and Alexander. How have you been? I had some free time, so I thought I would send you a message. And I have not forgotten . . . happy birthday, Father . . ."

Chapter Six

CERTAINLY, AT OTHER TIMES and in other places, Jean-Luc Picard had dined more elegantly. But he could not recall the last time he'd had a meal as satisfying as this one.

Between catching the damned fish, cleaning and preparing them with utensils improvised from rock and wood, then starting a fire with the most primitive techniques, dinner on Domarus wound up taking considerably more effort than sliding a tray out of a starship food synthesizer.

But I did it. He smiled to himself as he watched one of the day's catch sizzling on a stick propped above the campfire on a cross-brace made of tree branches. Then he leaned closer and squeezed a plum-sized piece of yellow fruit over the fish, letting the pulpy juice dribble down onto it.

Picard knew his own ancestry well, and he was aware that the French love affair with fine cuisine went back through recorded history, and probably predated that. As he savored the last bites of the fish he'd already cooked, Picard wondered about the origins of such regional characteristics. Was it all based on cultural indoctrination, or was it—as generations of Frenchmen had insisted—simply in the blood?

No matter. Nothing could prevent him from taking great pleasure in his ability to rise above the rudimentary needs of survival and turn this meal into something tasty. *I just hope there's nothing latently poisonous about all this . . .*

"Smells good."

The voice startled Picard and he nearly fumbled the fish in his hands. Then he spotted Captain Arit, out in the darkness across the campfire, hanging back on the fringe of the woods. *Damn—she's sneaky.* "Are you hungry?"

She circled part of the way around, but kept the fire between them. "No."

"Have you eaten?" He made an extra effort to sound friendly, even though he didn't really trust her, or her motivations.

"Some fruit," she said.

"There's plenty here for both of us."

"I'm a light eater."

Arit's arrival distracted him from his cooking long enough for the pleasing aroma of roasting fish to turn acrid as it began to burn. Just in time, Picard snatched it away from the flame. Though a bit more charred than he liked, it still looked edible. The damned fish had taken too much effort to catch—he was most certainly not going to discard any that were remotely edible. He sat back on the ground—and realized the Teniran woman had moved silently closer, now crouching not more than three meters away.

"I didn't help you catch them," she said. "In fact, I laughed at you."

"So?"

"So why are you so willing to share?" The reflection of the fire glinted in her pale green eyes.

"I caught more than I can eat. No point in wasting any of it." He held out the freshly cooked fish. She reached forward and took the stick from him, then immediately retreated again to her three-meter perimeter.

Her fangs flashed in the firelight as she tore into the crispy fish. Picard guessed she was a lot more hungry than she would admit.

"You surprise me, Picard," Arit said between bites.

"Oh? In what way?"

"Your survival skills didn't look especially sharp earlier today."

His mouth curled into a subtle smile. "Ah. Well . . . let's just call it trial and error."

"How did you get this to taste so good?"

"Nothing magical. Where I come from, on Earth, a place called France, cooking is almost a religion. Great chefs are like high priests protecting sacred mysteries," he said as he skewered another fish. As he continued, he seasoned it with fruit juice and pulp. "But satisfactory cooking isn't really mysterious at all. Care to try it for yourself?"

She frowned in abrupt annoyance. "Cooking isn't one of my skills. I was bred to be a ship captain."

"One doesn't necessarily preclude the other, Arit."

"It does where I come from. We Tenirans don't have the luxury of dabbling in hobbies as you humans do."

"We really don't know much about each other's societies," Picard said, hoping he could gingerly steer the conversation toward the point where they could actually exchange something more meaningful than small talk about fish.

It didn't work. Arit tensed and stood up, as if ready to fight—or flee. "If you think that a little food means I'll reveal all our secrets—"

"On the contrary," Picard said, "accepting food implies no obligation."

"That's what the powerful always tell the weak."

"Powerful? What makes you think we're powerful?"

"We know all about your Federation and your starships, Picard," Arit sneered.

Picard turned the fish over the fire, checking to assure it was cooking evenly. "You seemed to have no fear of my ship when you were threatening our shuttlecraft."

"Your presence here threatens us," said Arit sharply.

"You have no need to consider us a threat, Arit— though you may not believe me."

"I don't."

Deciding to try a more direct approach, Picard straightened up. "Allow me to remind you that we did not respond with force even though our shuttle was in mortal danger. Why do you want this planet so badly?" But she reacted by tossing the skewer to the ground and backing away, and he immediately regretted his direct inquiry. "Whatever your problem is, perhaps we can help—"

"Help? Help leads to betrayal," she said with a certainty Picard found both tragic and chilling. "We don't want your help."

"Captain Arit," he called. But she ignored him and slipped back into the dark woods beyond the campsite.

Neither captain noticed the single twinkling mote of crimson light quivering high over the campsite.

After hours of repair work that had proven mostly futile, dinnertime aboard the shuttlecraft *Onizuka* was understandably subdued. Wesley and Gina ate together at the front of the aft cabin, but seemed lost in private thoughts as they nibbled unenthusiastically on packaged rations. Data and Troi sat in the rearmost seats, though the android of course had no need for food. He occupied himself with a thorough analysis of the sensor information gathered earlier.

Only Ken chose to be physically by himself, slouched in the cockpit pilot's seat, absorbed in sporadic scribbling in a notepad. He didn't notice when Gina poked her head in from behind.

"What're you doing?"

Ken straightened abruptly, then realized she was peering at what he'd written on the pad. He flipped it face down, tried to look nonchalant, but succeeded only in looking uncomfortable. "Nothing."

"Come on, that wasn't some techie list." Gina squinted in disbelief. "What was it?"

"Just some notes."

"Looked like a poem to me."

He glared at her. "It was *not* a poem," he said, spacing his words deliberately.

"Suit yourself. I was just curious," Gina said with a shrug. She looked out the broad front windows at the cavern bathed in eerie illumination from the shuttle's running lights. "It sure does look pretty out there."

"Pretty?" His tone made it clear he regarded her description to be dubious at best.

"Yeah. But then I guess you'd rather be anywhere else but in a cave, right?" she teased.

"You really think you know me, don't you?" he said, annoyed at her insinuation. "Well, you don't."

With another shrug, she left him alone.

Dammit! Why do I always do that? he thought as he watched her go. *I could've shown her what I was writing . . . why didn't I? What the hell am I so afraid of? If she doesn't know what I'm really like, who's fault is that? It's mine!* He slouched down in the pilot's seat, wishing he could replay those last couple of minutes with Gina. She wasn't the first girl he'd liked this much, though there hadn't been many before. But they'd all turned out the same way . . . *nothing . . . just a big nothing.* Worse than that, most of the girls he'd liked had never even known it.

He just couldn't seem to figure out how to tell them. With some girls, he'd just freeze up and act like some kind of robot around them. Those were the ones who not only didn't know how he felt about them—they probably never even knew he existed.

A few times, though, it had been different. There'd at least been some conversation, something in common. *Maybe she'd be nice to me . . .* And Ken knew with a shudder what always seemed to happen next. He'd go overboard trying to be attentive and kind and thoughtful, the perfect formula for smothering any relationship before it could ever get off the launch pad. He couldn't help it, and he couldn't seem to do anything right. And he was afraid to even try.

Especially with someone like Gina. Not that there hadn't been a few nice moments here and there. *Just enough to give me some hope,* he thought bitterly. He glanced out the pilot's window, trying to see the beauty Gina saw out there in this confining cavern. Could there be beauty in a prison? In a tomb?

He knew that was the wrong attitude, but he couldn't help the way he saw the universe. Could he?

And besides, why do I always have to be the one to make the first move? It was the same dance every time, always doomed to failure. Why couldn't a girl like him first, just for a change? That would be so much easier, letting her lead the way. Then he would only have to respond . . . and maybe they'd just live happily ever after.

No, Gina didn't know him at all.

Of course, he knew why no girl ever seemed to like him first. *What is there to like? What could I possibly offer someone like Gina?* He wondered if Wesley ever had these same dark thoughts. Not likely.

He opened his notepad again and read the few lines he'd managed to scrawl in handwriting that was shockingly sloppy for a compulsively neat person. He didn't like what he'd done. *And who ever said you could write poetry anyway?*

In the aft compartment, Data turned away from the computer screen. "Counselor," he said softly, "I have been attempting to solve a puzzle and I wondered if I might have your input."

"If it's about those sensor readings you've been studying, I doubt I can provide much help."

"Actually, it is about a facet of human behavior."

"Oh?" Her eyebrows rose with interest. "What facet?"

Data cocked his head. "Fear . . . specifically, fear of death. Intellectually and quantitatively, I can understand it. But I cannot fathom the qualitative emotional aspects."

"Is this sudden interest related to our current situation?"

"Oh, it is not a sudden interest. It is a topic I have been curious about ever since I began serving with humans, especially humans facing potentially lethal dangers. I have done considerable reading on the subjects of fear and death."

"And that didn't help?"

"Yes and no. Biological death is the cessation of existence, and I can grasp why rational beings would fear that. It is not surprising that virtually all humanoid cultures have, to some degree, believed in various forms of altered or continued existence after death—"

"You mean, as in reincarnation or an afterlife of the soul—"

"Exactly," Data said, then paused as a pensive expression shadowed his face. "But for all the effort to duplicate the human life form in an artificially constructed mechanism such as myself, I am not human. There are distinctions that the most advanced programming and technology apparently cannot yet erase."

"Like the idea of having an indefinable soul?"

Data nodded sadly. "I am unable to accommodate that concept. And although I can cease to exist, much as a biological life-form can, I was not born with the knowledge that I had a finite life-span."

"Well, compared to us, you don't. Depending on what damage you sustain, and the level of repair technology, your life-span could very well be indefinite. But you're still programmed for self-preservation. How does that differ from the same biological instinct?"

"My imperative for self-preservation is consistent. I do not pass through the life phases which seem to alter human perceptions of themselves. For instance, I have observed that young humans are much more likely than adults to recklessly risk life and limb."

Deanna chuckled. "An observation probably made on a daily basis by every human parent in history."

"Yet, at a certain age, humans reject behaviors and activities they once undertook with little or no concern."

"I stopped climbing onto the roof of our shed," Deanna offered with a faraway look.

"Pardon?"

"We had a storage shed in our yard, and when I was six, I had this uncontrollable urge to see what the world looked like from a greater height. So I dragged a ladder out and climbed onto the roof of the shed."

"Did your parents object?"

"My father wanted to climb right up, haul me down and punish me."

"And your mother?"

"Mother had quite another reaction," Troi recalled with a knowing smile. "She knew the shed looked a lot higher to a six-year-old than it really was. Even if I fell off, I probably wouldn't do any great harm to myself. So she told me I could climb anywhere I wanted, if I could figure out how to get up there. She said it was good practice for life."

"Was it?"

"Yes. Though I've often wished I could be as bold now as I was then. Unless they're forced to do it, the young by nature do not worry about their own mortality."

"Nor do I, Counselor. And I am concerned that this deficiency prevents me from truly understanding what it is to be human—and detracts from my ability to be an effective leader in circumstances such as ours."

"Hmm." Troi frowned as she wrestled with Data's

dilemma, seeking a response that would make sense within an android's frame of reference. "Data, even with emphatic abilities like mine, it simply isn't possible to always know how someone else feels."

"Yet Captain Picard seems to know."

"Any good leader tries to be aware of the feelings of those around him, and the most effective way to do that is by keen observation. I've never met a better observer than you, Data. And as long as you've got that skill, you'll always be sensitive to others' fears and emotions, even those you don't quite understand. Trust me."

"Thank you, Counselor." Data stood. "Wesley, are you ready to begin our search for an exit from this cavern?"

"More than ready, Data."

The sensor scans they'd run earlier had shown the cave to be free of obvious dangers, with a breathable atmospheric mixture. Gina's structural analysis indicated the rock itself to be stable, with no detectable risk of collapse or cave-in. Now, equipped with phasers, tricorders and lanterns, Wes and Data opened the hatch and climbed out. In preparation for their exploration, they'd fashioned improvised safety tethers out of cord coiled inside dispensers mounted on their hips, and now they clipped the "home" end to utility nodes on the shuttle's side.

"Be careful," Troi said, standing in the open hatch. "If you feel disoriented in the tunnels, come back."

"We shall, Counselor. In any event, we will return in one hour," Data said. "Keep trying to contact the *Enterprise*."

Troi nodded and shut the hatch behind them.

Wesley swung his lamp around in a wide arc, getting his first really good look at the cavern. From outside the *Onizuka,* it looked and felt even more confining than it had through the shuttle windows. The dimensions of their rocky prison obviously hadn't changed —it was still configured like an uneven cone, varying from ten to fifteen meters in diameter, with an angled ceiling of dark, jagged stone and dripping stalactites ranging from a low point of just over four meters along one end all the way up to thirty meters at its asymmetrical peak.

To the human mind, however, the cave's actual size was only one factor in the equation. No matter how hard he tried, Wesley couldn't divorce those measurements from the knowledge that he and his companions were deep inside a planet, presumably surrounded by an unknown amount of more or less solid rock. Even in the unlikely event that they were able to get the engines and navigation systems up and working again, there was absolutely no way to fly the stranded shuttlecraft out of there. It seemed depressingly apparent that if the away team was going to escape, it would have to be on foot.

As Wes looked around, his lantern flashed past several tunnel openings. "Where should we start, Commander?"

Data scanned each tunnel with his tricorder, then paused. "This one appears to spiral upward." They started out, their tethers unreeling behind them.

"Uhh, Data, I—umm—I heard what you and Counselor Troi were talking about just before," Wesley said as they left the main cavern and entered the confines of the tunnel, shining their beams ahead to light the path.

"Oh? Do you have some thoughts you wish to share?"

"Yes, I do. Even though kids my age aren't supposed to be worried about their own mortality yet, I do think about death sometimes. Maybe it's because of my father dying when I was so young . . . when he was so young, too."

"Based on my research into human behavior, I believe that to be a natural reaction on your part, Wesley. Having to deal with death in such a direct manner is an experience that most of your peers do not share."

They ducked beneath a rock outcropping. "I sometimes wonder if my father had already reached that age where awareness of your own mortality starts to affect the way you see the world, whether it made him stop doing some of the risky things he did as a kid."

"From my reading in human psychology, that is likely."

Wes nodded. "That's what I figured. But then sometimes I wonder—if he knew he could die, why didn't he leave Starfleet and do something safer?"

"It is not possible to eliminate all risks, Wesley. His desire to serve in Starfleet and explore space must have outweighed his fears and concerns."

The tunnel narrowed, funneling them into single file with Data in the lead. As they moved forward, their lanterns cutting into the chilly, damp darkness, Wesley listened to the scuffing of their boots echoing off the rocks. He had to make a conscious effort to suppress his own fears.

He heard something behind them, like the groan of weakening rock . . . pebbles skittering down from above. He half-turned, expecting to see the start of a rockslide that would seal them in. He swept his lantern up, down, sideways. *Nothing . . . great imagination, Crusher . . .*

He jumped when an icy drop of water fell on his

forehead. Then he realized he'd fallen several strides behind Data and he hurried to catch up. *This is no place to get left behind.*

Somehow, his childhood dreams of exploring the final frontier had never seemed quite this claustrophobic. He felt the walls pressing in on him. He needed to hear his own voice.

"Data?"

"Yes?"

"What if . . . what if there's no way out of here?"

"If there was a way in, Wesley, there must also be a way out. It may not be *this* way . . . but there *is* a way, and there is no reason why we should not be able to find it."

Never in his life had Wesley Crusher wanted to believe anything as much as what Data had just said. "Do you really think so?"

"Indubitably."

Chapter Seven

"GINA! *Look out!*"

Inside the shuttle, Troi's heart raced as she heard Ken Kolker's bleat of alarm bloom into an explosion of echoes. Though strange caverns on alien worlds could scarcely be guaranteed as risk-free, she and Data had deemed the immediate area around the stranded shuttlecraft to be safe enough for limited exploration. And she knew it would be good for morale to keep the young away team members as busy as possible.

At the sound of Ken's warning shout, however, Deanna popped through the open hatch, fully expecting to see the aftermath of some horrible accident.

Instead, she saw Gina glaring at her companion, hands on her hips. "What is *with* you, Kenny?"

"I thought you were about to get crushed by a cave-in," Ken said, head hung in embarrassment.

"Cave-in?" Gina noticed Troi poised on the hatch sill and cast an annoyed glance toward her. "I'm chipping out some rock samples, a little dust and two pebbles rattle down from above me, and he thinks it's a cave-in."

"I was just being cautious," Ken protested.

"Cautious?"

"Yes, cautious—and I don't think there's any such thing as being too cautious, considering where we are right now."

Gina turned away, rolling her eyes. "Oh, pleeease."

Satisfied that no disasters loomed, Counselor Troi went back inside the shuttle. She wondered if Data and Wesley had found anything. Their hour of scouting was almost up, and Data was never late. They'd be returning soon.

With a bewildered shake of his head, Ken retreated to his own sample collection, concentrating on drippings from an impressive array of stalactites hanging down like fangs from the roof of some monstrous mouth.

"I'm sorry if I overreacted," Kenny muttered after a wordless stretch of five minutes or so.

"Forget it."

"You're probably thinking, 'Wesley wouldn't have gotten hysterical.' "

Gina glanced at him, genuinely caught off-guard by what seemed like a complete non sequitur. "Why would I think that?"

"I don't know. Because all the kids on the ship look up to him."

"Why shouldn't they look up to him? He's smart, he's responsible, he works harder than almost anybody in our classes. But he's not perfect, and he never claimed to be. Who knows how he would've reacted? But the truth is, I wasn't thinking about Wesley at all . . . until you mentioned him. All I was thinking

about was these samples . . . and getting out of here."
She tossed a handful of mineral chips into a collection
bag.

Ken blinked in surprise. "You were really thinking
about getting out of here? I figured you wouldn't mind
being marooned in here."

"Kenny," she said patiently, "I don't mind visiting
caves. But I don't really want to spend the rest of my
life stuck inside *this* one."

"Do you think we might . . . y'know . . . die here?"

"You might, 'cause I may kill you," she quipped,
then shrugged in clear discomfort as she realized that
Kenny seemed intent on pursuing a subject she'd
rather skip. "I don't know. I haven't really thought
about it."

"Not at all?" He obviously didn't believe her.

She hesitated. "Well . . . maybe a little. But not
seriously. Look, I'm sure we'll get out of here."

"But you really did think about it . . . about dying
in here?"

Gina sighed, wishing she could somehow take back
her tacit admission. Now that she'd been edged into
talking about it at all, this was not a topic over which
she really cared to linger. "I said I did . . . a little.
Why are you making such a big deal about it?"

"Because you've said you don't like thinking about
death."

Gina stared at him. "Most people don't, you know.
Why *should* I? I'm not as morbid as you."

"I'm not morbid," he insisted. "Death is part of
life."

"So is snoring, but I don't spend large portions of
my day contemplating that either."

The sound of advancing footfalls interrupted their
debate, and Data and Wesley emerged from the same

tunnel they'd entered on their search. Data's neutral expression revealed nothing, but the grim tightness of Ensign Crusher's jaw made it clear they'd failed to find a way out. Gina approached them.

"No luck?"

Without a word, Wes just shook his head.

Gina planted herself in front of Data. "Commander, there are lots of other tunnels. I want to be part of the next search team. *Nobody* knows caves like I do. If anybody can find a way out, *I* can."

"I can vouch for that, sir," Wes Crusher said with a nod. "She takes to caves like a Kavarian horn mole."

"Indeed." Data seemed impressed by the testimonial.

"Wesley," said Gina, basking in the unexpected praise, "that's one of the nicest things anybody's ever said about me."

Wesley's mouth twitched in mock horror. "Geez, I hope not."

"Very well, Gina," Data said. "You and I shall make another attempt to find an exit . . ."

"Thank you, sir!" She clapped her hands in anticipation. "I'm ready to go."

". . . after an adequate sleep period," Data said, completing his interrupted sentence. "We have had a long and difficult day and rest is required."

Gina let out a disappointed sigh, then smiled to herself as she remembered what it was like to be a little girl and have her parents tell her she couldn't go out and play because it was bedtime. That's pretty much what Data just did . . . Her warm feeling of nostalgia quickly chilled. She caught herself wondering, *Will I ever see my parents again?*

* * *

"Uh, Commander Riker, you're pacing," said Chief Engineer La Forge, watching the first officer cross back and forth in front of the big observation windows in the conference lounge.

Riker knew exactly what he was doing. He also knew why. Simple. He just didn't like to sit still. Not now, not ever. He couldn't begin to count the boyhood scoldings he had absorbed from teachers exasperated by his fidgeting. As he'd grown up, he'd concentrated on harnessing that unquenchable fount of nervous energy, channeling it, learning to skirt the ragged border separating bold action from recklessness. Sometimes the line was hard to find.

With a sheepish smile and a sigh, Riker dropped into a seat. "Geordi, I'm afraid patience is not exactly my strong suit. But I am better than I used to be, believe it or not. You know who's the most patient man I've ever met?"

"Captain Picard," Geordi said without an instant of hesitation, his words declaring a truth, not asking a question. He knew. So did everyone aboard the *Enterprise.*

"The man is a master," Riker agreed with a grin. "It took me a while to appreciate it, though. Remember when we all started aboard the *Enterprise?* We'd get into some pretty tight spots, and I would be sitting there on the bridge thinking, *Fire the damn phasers,* and he's sitting there, as cool as you please, like he's got forever to make a decision."

Geordi nodded. "Yeah, I know what you mean. That imperturbability of his did take some getting used to. Every now and then, I'd sort of remind myself, here we are serving with a living legend."

"I must admit to wondering once or twice whether

he was more legend than alive. But I learned something from observing the captain that I never quite realized before."

"What's that, sir?"

"That action doesn't have to be explosive to be effective—and the *first* solution isn't always the *best* solution."

Still, times like the present could push Riker's developing patience to the breaking point. The *Enterprise* had been orbiting Domarus Four for nearly a day. Not only was the shuttle still missing—so was Picard. Riker and his officers were proceeding in logical and orderly fashion . . . without result. He would gladly trade patience for a bolt of inspiration.

Unfortunately, there were no such thunderbolts in Geordi's latest sensor report now displayed on the table-top computer screen.

"I don't get this, Geordi," Riker said, staring at the data. "There's no indication of any life down there that bears even the remotest resemblance to human life. Why can't our sensors find the captain?"

Geordi's sigh betrayed his frustration. "Ever since we started searching, there's been an uneven but continuing increase in electromagnetic emissions surrounding Domarus Four."

"Any luck figuring out a source for that?"

"I'm sure it's something on or in the planet. But we can't pin it down to anything specific."

"Why not?"

"Because whatever it is, it's interfering with our scanners."

Riker rubbed his eyes. "Geordi, it's been a long day. As long as Captain Picard's missing, I'm not going to get much sleep. I don't get sleep, I get cranky. And believe me, you do *not* want to see me cranky."

"I believe you, Commander."

"I'm sure you do. Now is there anything you can do about the sensors?"

"If we can chart a predictable rate of increase for those electromagnetic emissions, we might be able to program a compensation curve. But first we have to try to get a handle on the emissions rate, and that'll take time and—"

"Patience," Riker finished, an ironic glint in his eye. "I'll try to keep that in mind."

It had been dark for almost two hours now, and Picard rolled onto his back, crinkling the leaves he'd gathered as a rudimentary mattress to cushion the hard ground beneath him. A faint breeze whispered through the treetops bordering the clearing, and Picard's crackling fire cast a dancing glow across the campsite. Above him, the stars twinkled with piercing brightness.

The constellations were not those of Earth, but Picard had seen many an alien sky, and he had learned firsthand that the heavens teemed with life. From where he lay now, he might not be able to pick out Orion the Hunter or the crab or the lion or the Great Bear, but he had been a star traveler long enough to think of *all* the stars—even those he couldn't name—as friends.

Not that he'd always regarded the stars so warmly. With a private smile, he recalled the first time he'd slept out of doors, when he was four—in the yard of the Picard home, with his playmate Louis, brother Robert and Robert's friend Claude.

"Claude . . . what a troublemaker," Picard said aloud, addressing the stars with a rueful shake of his head. Claude had told little Jean-Luc that the stars were tiny fireballs waiting to fall on him and burn him to a crisp while he slept. *And what did my big brother do?*

Before he could answer his own question, Picard felt the ground shudder beneath him, as if some distant giant had taken one step and paused. Then, stillness.

"Robert went on to convince me that thousands of children were incinerated each year by voracious falling stars," he murmured with a chuckle—a chuckle cut short by a new tremor, more forceful than the first.

This one did not stop. As the distant rumble rolled closer, Picard sat up suddenly and recognized the oscillation of a major planetquake building under him. Loose stones skittered down the hillsides bounding his campsite. Was he about to be buried under a landslide?

He got to his feet, but the quake's wildly increasing magnitude threw him to the ground—ground that heaved and split around him as a sinkhole yawned open, and the quake roared in his ears. With frantic hands, he clawed for a hold on soil and grass that kept collapsing beneath him, tumbling into the widening rift. Despite his struggle to escape, he knew he was being sucked down, and the dirt falling into the chasm after him quickly began to bury him.

Then, as spontaneously as it had begun, the roaring stopped. Picard forced his reeling mind to orient itself. He was on his back, head pitched down, half-entombed. He opened his eyes and blinked into the soil resting against his face. He could still see the stars. He spat out a mouthful of dirt, and forced his arms up toward the sky, hoping he could dig his way out. But every motion brought more dirt down into the hole, down onto his body. *Can't move—can't get out—don't panic!*

Then he felt something hard and rough against his outstretched hand, and he heard an insistent voice from above.

"Grab it, Picard."

Arit . . . where the hell did she come from?

Taking care to limit his movements and not bring more soil cascading down, he obeyed and closed both hands around the sturdy tree branch extending down to him.

"Hold it tight."

He applied all his remaining strength to that grip, then felt himself being hauled out of his grave. The dirt around his legs tugged back as if fighting his release. Finally, he was pulled free and he used his knees to push himself away from the sinkhole. Arit, who'd been stretched out on her stomach, got to her feet and stepped back carefully until they were both back on solid ground.

Then they both collapsed, chests heaving from the strain of the rescue.

Hoisting himself up on one elbow, Picard spat out another mouthful of grit and tried to speak. But the best he could manage was a hoarse whisper. "Thank you, Captain."

"We are even, Picard."

"Even? I—I don't understand."

"For the food," Arit said.

"Food? There was no price for that food."

"There's always a price."

"In that case, Captain Arit, our trade was hardly even. All I gave you was a meal. You . . . you gave me my life."

Neither captain knew if they were truly on safe

ground, nor if any aftershocks would come along to swallow them up. But they were too exhausted to move and they fell asleep where they lay.

And neither one heard the atonal, distant jangling that filled the air as a pair of twinkling splinters of light materialized, hovering a meter apart in the night sky above the ruined campsite. And even if they had, they would not have known that the two points of light, one a deep gold, the other an angry crimson, were speaking to each other, in a way no human could understand.

The golden one flared. :**You should not have done this, Mog.**:

:**I was only doing what we are meant to do, Ko—Shaping the World. They should not have been in the way.**:

:**You knew they were here. You could have been more careful. This place did not have to be shaped at this moment,**: the gold one said.

:**And who is at fault, Ko? I am not. You should never have brought them here. These things should be destroyed.**:

:**No! They must not be damaged. They are Life.**:

Now the crimson one spun furiously. :**How dare you call them Life! They are not like us—they contaminate our World—they are not like us—they are not Life.**:

:**You show your ignorance, Mog. Just because they are not like us does not mean they cannot be Life.**:

:**Then why have we not seen them before? Tell me that, oh Brilliant One,**: said Mog sarcastically. :**Were they hiding in the rocks?**:

:**They may have come from other than our World, Mog.**:

:That is blasphemy! There is NOTHING other than our World! This is all that exists.:

:Is your mind really so small, Mog? How wondrous it must be to know everything there is to know. Do you know what lies in the darkness beyond what we can see? Many of us agree with me—many believe that much lies beyond the Great Darkness.:

:You should not have brought these things here,: Mog repeated, his fiery shape spinning threateningly.

:That is not your decision,: Ko said. :This is my Communion—my vision will lead.:

:The Elders may differ—especially now that you speak of demon worlds out in the Great Darkness. They are not pleased with what you did before the rest of us awoke from Interval—taking these two things from their containers—holding the other things and their small container inside our World—:

:They are not THINGS!: Ko exploded. :They are Life, and I will prove it.:

:How?: Mog challenged derisively. :They do not have the intelligence to speak to us.:

:Maybe they speak differently. I will find out how to communicate with them, and I will PROVE that you are wrong, Mog.:

:Very well. Because this is your Communion, I will give you two cycles, Ko. If you have not taught these things to speak by then, I will destroy them as the poisonous things they are, before they can taint our World any more than they already have.:

:No!: Ko flared in protest. :Two cycles may not be enough.:

:Two cycles is all you will get. A majority of the Elders support me. If you do not agree, you will be removed, Ko, and the things will be snuffed out NOW.:

:Then I am forced to agree. But I WILL do what I say, Mog—just to prove you wrong. And now I say it will not even take me two cycles.:

The confrontation ended when the crimson glimmer of energy flared forcefully and winked out. Left alone, the gold one dimmed and fluttered low over the sleeping bodies of Picard and Arit, like an impossibly tiny star fallen from the cosmos. Ko wondered what they really were. And she wondered if she had let Mog force her into a challenge she could not win.

Mog was right about one thing—to many of their population, Ko's ideas were blasphemy. The majority did believe without reservation that their World was everything; nothing else existed. The very thought that their faith might be wrong, or incomplete, terrified many. But not all.

It was true that they had never directly encountered anything that called their faith into question. But some had questioned it nonetheless, Ko among them.

We are of this place, said the Orthody, the canon of the faith. *We cannot leave the World. We must remain here for all Communions to come. That is truth. So, then, why would the Creator bother to make other worlds? If we cannot go to them, they do not exist.*

Ko found it hard to argue against the Orthody. But she still had her lingering doubts—*there may be things of which we simply do not know . . . if we do not ask questions, how will we ever know?*

Such inquiries were not welcome. But Ko felt they had to be made, and she had decided long ago that when her turn came to lead the Communion, she would not shrink from the task. Not that she'd had any idea how to go about testing the Orthody. After all, it was a physical fact that Ko and those like her were bound to their World. They could not escape it, could not explore beyond it.

And, as far as they knew, nothing from beyond the Great Darkness had ever come to them.

Until now. The long rest known as Interval had not yet been due to end, but something had intruded. Some force had jostled Ko awake early. And she had risen and seen the things she believed to be Life, moving about on her World.

But by the time she'd found them, they were already about to leave. She'd tried to speak to them, but they did not understand. Nor did she understand the sounds they made. But she was certain, beyond all doubts, that they were an answer to her questions. She desperately wanted—needed—to communicate with them, whatever they were. But how?

She hadn't wanted to hurt them, and could not voluntarily stop them. Sadly, she had been watching them go when the small container became ensnared by the larger container. And even though she had no common language with the live things, she had been astonished to feel the colors of hostility, the shades of danger. Ko considered that revelation to be certain proof that she and all these live things shared much despite being such different forms of life.

Then the second large container had arrived. The colors had darkened and she was afraid to wait any longer. With no time to think, Ko had acted on her first impulse—preserve the few in immediate danger! So she took the small container and put it in a place of safety.

From the beginning, her only desire had been to gain time to establish contact with these new Lives. She had to learn to understand them, to get them to understand her. What was so wrong with that? This was not some hypothetical debate. They were here—and Mog and his kind could no longer ignore the existence of something they had never known before.

But Mog and his faction *could* destroy them. And they would, unless Ko could accomplish what she'd set out to do . . . to make this one dream real.

Chapter Eight

"HEY, KEN—do you need some help?" Wesley Crusher leaned his lanky body out through the shuttle's side hatch, looking across the cavern to where Ken was busy collecting additional rock and mineral samples. Wes waited for a reply, then frowned when none came. *He must have heard me . . .*

Then again, Ken Kolker had a way of getting so wrapped up in whatever he was doing that it was quite possible that a volcanic eruption might escape his notice until molten lava steamed past his toes. So Wes hopped down and walked over to where Ken squatted on one knee, carefully chipping a few small chunks out of a blue mineral vein running irregularly along the cave wall. "Anything I can help you with?"

"I heard you the first time," Kenny muttered without looking up.

"Oh. Well, is there?"

"No."

"You sure? I just thought—"

"If I wanted any help, I'd have said yes, now wouldn't I?" said Ken, with a distinctly chilly edge in his voice.

"Sure. I guess." Wes considered a retreat to the shuttle, but decided to press forward with small talk. He really had no idea what was bothering his friend. "Data and Gina should be back soon. Do you think they'll find a way out?"

Ken's eyes remained on his work. "How am I supposed to know?"

"Is there something wrong? If there is, we've obviously got plenty of time to talk about it."

"Nothing's wrong, Wesley."

"Are you sure?" Wes asked again, not really certain that persistence was his best choice.

Ken answered with a derisive snort as he glared up at Wesley. "You don't have a clue, do you?"

Wesley blinked in surprise at the current of sudden hostility running beneath Kenny's answer. "A clue about what?" His mental reflexes told him to back off, but his smattering of command training reminded him to resist that easier course. It didn't take a boy genius, or any other kind of genius for that matter, to grasp the fact that there was an obvious problem here, and it had to be dealt with.

Ken turned back to his rock chipping. "You know what I sometimes feel like calling you?"

"What?"

"Beemots."

A perplexed furrow wrinkled Wesley's brow. He had no idea what Kenny was talking about. "Beemots?"

"Yeah. B-M-O-T-S," Ken said, spelling out the letters. "Big Man on the Starship." Ken stood up and brushed the coating of dust off his knees.

Wes wasn't sure whether to be hurt or mad. Actually, he felt a little of both. "Why?"

"Because you're an ensign with a uniform."

Wesley's arms folded defensively across his chest. He felt an embarrassed flush coloring his face. "Hey, I'm not the first person in history to receive a field commission."

"You are on this ship." Ken paused, as if weighing options—should he continue, or drop it here? He decided to go with a touch of deliberate nastiness. "Do you ever wonder if you got that field commission because your mother is buddy-buddy with Captain Picard?"

Wesley felt his concern for whatever was bugging Kenny getting crowded out by his own emotions, which skidded distinctly toward anger. But he made a deliberate effort to keep it out of his voice. "Is that what you think?"

The shorter teen frowned as he formulated a careful answer, delivered with a shrug. "No, I guess not. You're too nice a guy, and I know you earned what you got. But that doesn't mean I'm not jealous."

"Jealous? Of what?" Wesley shook his head, trying to understand.

"Ask Gina."

"Gina? What does this have to do with her? Are you saying *she's* jealous of me?"

Ken snickered. "You really don't get it, do you? You know, Crusher, for a smart guy, you can be awfully dense sometimes."

"I never said I couldn't be. How about giving me a hint."

"Everybody sees how Gina looks at you."

"How she looks at me? Is that what this is about? Gina and I are just friends."

"Oh, sure you are."

"We are," Wes insisted.

"But she notices you . . . constantly. The only way she'd ever notice me is if I singlehandedly got us out of here."

"Maybe that's the way out, Commander," Gina called back over her shoulder. She marched several strides ahead of Data, deeper down a narrow passage splitting off the main tunnel. "Can't we at least try?"

Her android escort scanned ahead into the darkness with both his flashlight and tricorder. "I am afraid this branch ends just like the others did, Gina. Besides, we have been searching for almost two hours. It is time we turned back. You will need to rest."

"But I'm not tired, Commander. Pleeeease?" she begged as she turned back to him, her stance a mixture of adolescent petulance and adult urgency.

"It is possible that we will find an exit to the surface—and we shall continue our search. But not here, and not now. It is time to return to the shuttle," he said, more firmly this time.

Gina's shoulders slumped. "Yes, sir."

Wesley Crusher sat by himself, hunched in the shuttle cockpit, staring at the pilot's console but not really seeing it. He'd left Kenny outside in the cave and come back to the ship to try to make some sense of their conversation. *Is that how everybody sees me, or just Kenny?*

"Wesley?"

The sound of Deanna Troi's voice behind him caught him by surprise and he sat up abruptly, managing to ram his kneecap into the console—"Owww!"

—as he turned to see her standing in the mid-ship hatchway.

"Sorry," she said. "I didn't mean to startle you. But you looked like a young man with something serious on his mind. Is it anything you want to talk about?"

"It's nothing. I'm okay," he said with a halfhearted shrug. Then he winced and rubbed his throbbing knee. "At least I was," he added, an ironic trace of a smile curling one corner of his mouth.

"Are you sure you don't want to talk? It appears that all my previously scheduled appointments have been canceled for today."

He laughed in spite of his reflective mood, but the laugh faded quickly, replaced by a sigh. Counselor Troi leaned against the other cockpit couch. Then he told her what Ken had said to him.

"Which bothers you more," she asked, "the part about Ken being jealous of your being an ensign, or the part about Gina?"

"The field commission part I understand, and I can deal with that. When the captain made me an ensign, I figured if I didn't flaunt the uniform, and if I worked hard, none of the other kids would mind. I really don't think anybody does, and I don't think Ken does either. I think that was just his way of getting into the other thing."

"Gina."

He nodded. "I just don't get it, Deanna. I never thought girls thought I was anything special."

"What *did* you think?"

"What do you mean?"

"How did you see yourself?"

Wesley's long eyelashes fluttered in embarrassment. "I don't know. Kind of a bookworm, I guess. I always

109

felt kind of uncomfortable around girls—I never knew what to say. I always wished I could be more like Commander Riker."

Troi smiled slightly. "He does have a way with women. But how do you know you don't have your own natural way?"

"Me? I don't think so. I always thought I was too thin . . . and . . . I was never the best at sports. And I'm not exactly the life of the party. It's not that I'm down on myself—I know I've got my share of good qualities, and I'm not surprised when a girl likes me. But I can't understand why anyone would think that girls're falling all over me."

Counselor Troi slipped into the other cockpit seat, then swiveled to face Wesley. "Everything is relative. Has it occurred to you that perhaps Ken looks up to you the way you look up to Commander Riker?"

His eyes widened in disbelief. "You're kidding, right?"

She chuckled. "No, I'm not. You and Ken seem to share a problem that is quite common and perfectly natural for people your age."

"Insecurity, right?"

"I thought I was the counselor here," she quipped. "Look, Wesley, feelings of insecurity are nothing to be ashamed of, as long as they are kept in perspective. It is entirely natural for young people to worry about what others think of them."

"Even Betazoids?"

"Why shouldn't we?"

"Because you're empathic. You'd know what other people thought of you."

She nodded. "Exactly—and there were lots of times when I would have preferred not knowing. There still are." Troi leaned closer to him, her voice dropping to a conspiratorial hush. "Can I tell you a secret?"

"I guess," he said uncertainly.

"When I was a child, I was acutely aware that I was only half Betazoid. I knew my empathic abilities would never be the same as other Betazoid children. And that's what made *me* insecure."

"Did the other kids tease you about being half human?"

"A few did. But it wasn't what *they* thought that bothered me. It was what I *thought* they thought, even when they didn't." Troi pursed her lips with bemused recollection. "As a result, I became rather shy, and people mistook shyness for remoteness—and that reinforced a cycle of isolation. All I really wanted was for other children to accept me for *me*. Yet my own fears created a barrier that kept them from doing that."

"Is that why you became a counselor?"

"Part of the reason, yes. I wanted to do something that would help people understand one another—and themselves—a little better."

"So . . . what should I do?"

"There aren't any magic solutions, Wesley. I think you are well aware of your gifts and talents—as well as your weaknesses. That sort of special self-awareness will more than likely carry you over any peer-group bumps in the road to adulthood. Besides, you're almost there. Just be what you are, and the chances are rather good that others will see you that way."

"That's it?"

"Pretty much," she said with a soft smile.

"Hey!" It was Kenny from outside the shuttlecraft. "They're back."

Wesley and Deanna went to the hatch and hopped down to the cavern floor. One look at Gina made it obvious she and Data had not found a way out.

"No luck?" said Wesley.

"If by that you mean, did we discover an exit," Data said, "no, we did not."

"But it *is* out there," Gina said, glancing at the faces around her. "I *know* it is. It *has* to be. And I *am* going to find it."

"What did you find that's so urgent?" asked William Riker as he strode from the turbolift onto the bridge, joining Geordi and Worf at the security chief's tactical station. Only when Worf stepped aside did Riker notice the young woman standing behind the burly Klingon. She wore science-officer blue and had chestnut bangs falling just above her doe eyes. Riker's own eyes twinkled. "Lieutenant Casby—geologist, right?"

"Yes, sir," she answered, a slight tinge of red shading her cheeks. "You have a good memory."

"For memorable people."

Geordi cleared his throat. "I hope you weren't sleeping when we called, were you, Commander?"

"Not much," Riker said, a humorless smile on his lips.

"I didn't think so."

"So what've you got?"

Geordi led the way to one of the science consoles at the back of the bridge and keyed a computer display. "What we've got is . . . this."

A three-dimensional graphic grid appeared on the screen above the console. The visual and the labeling made it clear to Riker that he was looking at a

112

topographical depiction of a section of one Domaran continent.

Geordi confirmed that—northern hemisphere, temperate zone, including the base-camp site of the missing shuttlecraft, which was indicated on the grid by a blinking green dot.

"Looks like a flat plain," Riker said.

"Grasslands, actually," said Casby, stepping forward. "At least, that's what it looked like yesterday, sir."

Riker's eyes narrowed. "What do you mean, that's what it looked like yesterday? What does it look like today?"

"Computer," Casby said crisply, "display update."

The image of the flat prairie was replaced by what looked like a small mountain range, five peaks of varying sizes, all sharing a similar profile with moderately steep sides and rounded tops. All seemed to be free of the craggy irregularities associated with natural weathering and the geologic forces which commonly shaped planet surfaces.

Riker noticed other minor changes in the landscape—a valley where rolling hills had been, and a previously straight river now coiling itself like a snake around the base of the mountains. But the mountains themselves were the most blatant difference. "Casby, are you telling me these weren't there yesterday but they are today?"

"That's right, sir."

"But that's impossible," the first officer said. "Mountain ranges don't form overnight."

Geordi La Forge shrugged. "Normally, no. But this one apparently did. Computer, display both scans, full view."

Following La Forge's command, the computer first ran a simulated topographical fly-over of the plain, then of the new mountains. After a repeat comparison, Riker leaned against the console and folded his arms over his chest. "There's got to be some rational explanation for this. Maybe a sensor malfunction?"

Geordi shook his head. "That was the first thing we thought of, Commander. Everything checks out as nominal."

"But I thought the interference from those energy patterns prevented accurate readings."

"They do, to some extent," Geordi said. "It all depends on the overall energy output of whatever we're scanning. For instance, picking up something like Captain Picard's life-form telemetry—well, that we can't seem to do. But even with the static, we didn't have any trouble registering a major seismic upheaval."

Riker glanced at Casby. "Seismic upheaval?"

"Yes, sir," she said. "And with no apparent cause."

"Do you have an explanation?"

"Not an explanation, exactly, sir. We haven't picked up any tectonic instability—or any volcanic activity. Nothing that would lead us to believe something like this"—she tapped the computer screen—"could form so quickly. These mountains resemble ranges that take a good hundred-thousand years to form through natural geological processes."

Gazing at the graphic, Riker nodded slowly. "So, in your opinion, these were not formed by natural processes."

"In my opinion, that's right, sir."

"Commander," said Worf, who had been silent throughout the briefing, "if Captain Picard is down there in the midst of geological chaos, he is clearly in grave danger."

"No argument there, Worf," Riker agreed. "And if Mother Nature's not responsible for all this, then who the hell is?"

His uniform dirty and tattered, Captain Picard stood on a knoll above the fissure that had nearly swallowed him up the night before. The morning air had a refreshing snap to it, chilly enough to make his breath condense. He had managed to get perhaps five hours of sleep, and he felt not at all rested. Nearly every muscle in his body ached from his life-and-death struggle. *What I wouldn't give for a nice, long massage right now . . .*

Despite the twinge in his shoulder as he raised his arm, he shaded his eyes with one hand and gazed into the soft yellow light of sunrise. He expected that the day would warm up rather nicely before long. But he wasn't looking at the sun. His attention was focused on something silhouetted against the sky—the rounded peaks of a mountain range out on the horizon.

A mountain range that had not been there the day before.

"Interesting," said a voice behind him.

He turned to find Captain Arit coming up the slope just behind him, her golden face and dark mane streaked with dirt. "I could swear there was an open plain out there yesterday," he said. "No mountains."

"Maybe they were hidden behind fog or clouds," she offered.

"That does not seem likely. There was hardly a cloud in the sky yesterday. Besides, I'd guess they're only a few kilometers from here."

She came up beside him, blowing out a scornful snort as she protected her eyes from the brightening sunlight with her arms folded across her brow. "So what are you suggesting, Picard—that those mountains just rose up in a matter of hours?"

"Scientifically, I would say that is preposterous." He rubbed some caked mud off his cheek. "But Domarus Four seems to be full of surprises. No geological theory I know of would explain it, but the quake we experienced last night could be related to the formation of those mountains."

Arit's eyes twitched in a skeptical glance. "I'd like to see the proof of that."

"Then perhaps we should see if there is any such proof to be found."

"You mean go out there?"

"We seem to have no other pressing business," Picard noted. "And if last night is any example, it might be to our mutual benefit to stick together."

"Together." Arit's jaws quirked thoughtfully, letting one fang slip over her lower lip. "If we'd been together at your campsite last night, we would have both been buried alive. I'm not sure I shouldn't go my own way."

Picard shrugged. "Suit yourself, then. But I am going to take a closer look at those mountains."

Nothing worth taking along had escaped the previous night's brush with death, so he simply headed down the slope before them, taking advantage of the bracing chill of morning and hiking briskly toward the newborn mountains. He hadn't gone far when he noticed Arit following, perhaps fifty meters back over his left shoulder. He purposely slowed a bit, to see if she would match his speed and keep her distance. Instead, she maintained the initial pace, and it didn't take long for her to catch up and converge with him. They walked on in silence—

—until they noticed a hesitant chiming riding on the breeze, distant and dissonant. The sounds seemed to be following, and catching up, just as Arit had done.

Then a swash of colors materialized before them, flitting about the two starship captains as if the colors, too, were coasting on the currents of the wind. Arit began to bolt, but Picard grabbed her arm.

"Wait a moment, Arit."

"Picard! Let's get away from here." She wrenched out of his grip—but she did not flee.

He stood his ground, twisting and glancing about as the sheer streamers danced around them. The strange chiming enveloped them now, ringing with rising insistence. Picard could feel the sounds, and something compelled him to respond. But how?

Now the colors wrapped him and Arit inside their touchless embrace, and he felt lightheaded. He did not know if the sparkles of pure light he saw hovering over them were real, or optical illusions. But his skin began to tingle. Reality began to dissolve—and a moment later, Picard and Arit were gone from the surface of Domarus Four, leaving only the sparkles shivering in the cool morning air.

Chapter Nine

REALITY REINSTATED ITSELF as the iridescent swirl of colors deposited Captains Picard and Arit in a gloomy and dank corridor. A ship's corridor, Picard guessed, but certainly not *his* ship. He saw an easing of the taut muscles around Arit's mouth, and there seemed little doubt that they must be aboard her vessel, the *Glin-Kale*.

The colors lingered about them for a few heartbeats, like fading party ribbons, accompanied by the now-familiar jangling, sounding somehow like a distant musical question mark. Then, as before, sounds and colors simply winked out of existence.

"Home," Arit sighed softly.

Not much of a home, Picard thought as he looked around. The short stretch of corridor was filled with Tenirans worn and weary, huddled together against the curving walls, their meager belongings gathered around them. To Picard, they looked very much like refugees—*but refugees from what?* he wondered.

"Captain Arit," Picard began, "we—"

The sudden hoot of an alert horn cut him off. Overhead, illumination bars recessed into the ceiling began flashing sequentially in red. Arit whirled and broke into a run.

"Picard—this way!"

As he trailed her past the tattered people crowded into the passageway, Picard thought it strange that no one else seemed to react to the alert. He saw nothing but a numb resignation on their faces, as if such crises were nothing new, and nothing they could do anything about.

Arit and Picard rounded a corner and raced up a ramp, finally reaching a hatch jammed half-open. The Teniran captain cursed and squeezed through. Picard followed and found himself on what he guessed to be the bridge of the *Glin-Kale*. If he had been a man prone to claustrophobia, this cramped chamber would certainly have provoked a cold sweat. Compared to the bright, spacious command center of the *Enterprise,* Arit's bridge was a dim and Spartan place. A half-dozen shabbily clothed officers hunched over various consoles, all of which looked like they had been battered and patched dozens of times over, with repair-access covers missing, wiring hanging out, gerry-rigged circuit boards jammed where they clearly did not belong.

No one seemed to be paying any attention to him, but Picard couldn't help wondering if he was now a prisoner of the Tenirans.

An older officer leaning wearily on a walking stick stood near the command chair on a raised center pedestal and faced his commanding officer as she stepped up to him. Despite the insistent blaring of the alert horns, Arit took a moment to give his arm a squeeze.

"Good to have you back, Cap'n," Jevlin said.

She managed a faint hint of a smile. "You didn't think I'd leave you in command forever, did you?"

"I certainly hoped not."

"I'm sure the rest of the crew agrees," she teased. Then she squared her shoulders. "Now, Jevlin, how about telling me what's going on here?"

"It's the power core, Cap'n. The reactor chambers—"

"Oh, no—not again."

"'Fraid so. The—the magnetic seals are failing."

Arit slumped into her seat, closing her eyes for a pained moment as she let her head flop against the headrest. "That's it then." She straightened up, her face again tight with strain. "Chief Naladi said if they degraded any further, there'd be nothing left to repair."

"But we've got to *try,* Cap'n." The old officer tried his best to sound gallant, determined to ward off Arit's creeping pessimism. "Cap'n—*please*—we're all that's left of Tenira. Don't let 'er go like this."

"I don't want to, but I don't see a lot of choices. It looks like we've finally run out of threads and wishes, my old friend," Arit said in a somber voice.

Picard watched from the back of the bridge. He may have been unsure of his status—prisoner or guest—but he was certain he could not let the Tenirans sink without making one last attempt to help them. He stepped forward and spoke up. "How much time do you estimate until your reactors go critical?"

Jevlin measured him with a long glance. "Why should we tell you?"

"Because we may be able to help you."

"Cap'n," said Jevlin, "why did you bring him here?"

Arit and Picard exchanged a look. "Jevlin," she said, "I didn't. I don't even know why *I'm* here. At this point, I think it's safe to answer Picard's question."

"Cap'n!" The old Teniran pounded his walking stick on the deck. "We can't trust him. You *know* that—we can't trust anyone but ourselves."

Arit looked at the captain of the *Enterprise* with a defeated helplessness in her eyes. "It's our way, Picard. It wasn't always." She took a deep breath. "But it is now."

Picard shook his head gravely. "Arit, I do not know what has happened to your people because you've chosen not to tell me. Nor do I know what ordeals have caused this automatic mistrust of every stranger you meet. What I *do* know is this—your ship is in critical condition. For whatever my word may be worth to you, I promise that this offer of help will not lead to betrayal."

"Words," she said, without much conviction. "We've heard them before. They're as good as lies."

"Then let me put it to you this way. What have you got to lose? What is at stake here?"

Captain Arit stood and frowned, desperately searching Picard's eyes for truth. "Five thousand lives. The last of what we were . . . what we are."

"All right," he said quickly, "you are *certain* to lose all that if you do nothing. Do you want to die in space—on this ship—homeless?"

"We *have* a home," Jevlin spat. *"This* planet is our home. We can beam everyone down and—"

Picard silenced him with a glare. "You know as well as I do that you have neither the power nor the time to transport five thousand people."

"He's right about that, Jevlin," Arit said. "So answer his question. How much time until the core goes?"

"Cap'n—" Jevlin protested.

"Tell him!"

The ferocity of her order caught Jevlin by surprise and he fell back a reflexive step, his defiance wilting. "Thirty minutes . . . maybe an hour."

Picard faced Arit. "If you are willing to guarantee safe passage, I can have my engineer transport over here with a diagnostic team. Perhaps there's enough time to save the *Glin-Kale*." He knew if fate ever placed him in Arit's position, he would go to almost any lengths to preserve his ship and crew. As he searched her troubled expression for a sign, he could only hope that she shared this protective instinct he believed common to all ship commanders.

"And what conditions're you placing on this offer?" Jevlin demanded, his voice tight with suspicion.

"None. A simple truce—and we both lower our shields as a demonstration of good faith."

"Then how d'you know you can trust *us?* How d'you know we won't take you and your engineers and hold you?"

"I do not know for certain," Picard said with an unwavering gaze. "But I am willing to take that chance, Mr. Jevlin."

Captain Arit sank back into her seat again, her conflict showing all too clearly in her eyes. Then she swiveled away from Picard and Jevlin.

"Whatever you and your people have been through, it has obviously been a hard road," Picard said from behind her. "To have come all this way—only to fail here? Do you really want that to be your epitaph, Captain?"

122

She shut her eyes and covered her face with her hands. And she sat without a word. The confined bridge became silent as her officers awaited her decision.

"Gods forgive me," she finally whispered. Then she turned, and stood face to face with Picard. "Help us, Picard."

Lieutenant Worf glanced up from the tactical console above and behind the command well of the *Enterprise* bridge. "Commander Riker, incoming message from the *Glin-Kale*. Visual signal."

Riker got up from the command seat. "Let's see it, Worf. Main viewer."

An instant after Riker's order, the deceptively tranquil face of Domarus was replaced on the viewscreen by the Teniran bridge—and the startling image of Captains Arit and Picard standing side by side, their faces and uniforms still smudged with dirt.

"Captain!" Riker blurted, relief and concern clashing in his voice. He sensed Worf leaning forward behind him, and knew the Klingon security chief would be more than a little anxious to get the captain safely back aboard the *Enterprise*.

"Number One," Picard said with an ironic nod of greeting. He was well aware of the shock value of his sudden—and bedraggled—appearance.

"Are you all right, sir?"

"Quite all right, Commander."

"Begging your pardon, sir—but what the *hell* are you doing over there?"

"No time to explain now. Is Mr. La Forge there?"

Geordi strode down from the engineering alcove at the back of the bridge and joined Riker. "Right here, sir."

"Good. Commander La Forge, the Teniran ship is in critical need of engine repairs. I want you to transport over here with your best team of diagnostic propulsion experts—"

Riker took a step forward, his posture wary. "Captain, I don't know any way to say this except to be blunt. Are you being forced to make this request?"

"I am not a prisoner, if that's what you mean, Number One," Picard said, spreading his hands in a gesture of reassurance. "I have no way to prove that to you, except to say that Captain Arit and I have agreed to a truce. All shields down. And, based on the condition of their vessel, I do not believe the Tenirans currently present a threat to the *Enterprise.*"

"Mr. Worf," Riker said over his shoulder, without turning away from the big viewer, "confirm Teniran shield status."

"Their shields are down, sir," the Klingon rumbled.

Riker knew that tone of voice—Worf clearly did not trust the Tenirans and neither did he. *What the hell is going on here?* He had no reason to disbelieve the captain's statement, but neither did he have any reason to accept it.

"Will," Picard said urgently, "I understand your skepticism, but there is no time to waste."

Orders or no, Riker wasn't ready to fold. "Captain, you've been missing for almost twenty-four hours— and now you turn up on the *Glin-Kale,* out of the blue, without explanation. We have no idea if you're under duress, or even brainwashed. Under these circumstances, it's my *job* to be skeptical, isn't it?"

"It is," Picard said, his jaw muscles twitching the way they did when he had to make a grudging admission.

"Captain, are you giving me a direct order to send Geordi over there?"

"No, Number One," Picard said, advancing toward the viewer. "I am not. Compliance with this request is entirely at your discretion."

With that reply, the tension in Riker's posture reduced a notch. But he still wasn't ready to comply. "Are you free to return to the *Enterprise,* sir?"

"I believe I am." Picard turned to Arit with an apologetic smile. "My first officer is . . ."

". . . obviously very well-trained and absolutely correct," Arit said with an understanding fraction of a smile. "Commander Riker, our need for assistance is all too real. Captain Picard's offer is entirely voluntary. And to answer your question, he is free to return to your ship. I'm sure you've confirmed that our defensive shields are down. If you need further proof, transport him back to the *Enterprise* now, if you wish."

"Captain Picard," Riker said, "stand by for transport."

Picard turned to Arit. "Captain, I *will* have our engineers here within five minutes."

"If you do, you do. If you don't, you don't," the Teniran said with a fatalistic shrug. "At this point, Captain, I have accepted our fate, whatever it may be."

With a grim frown, Picard turned back toward the viewer. "All right, Number One. Beam me over."

Riker called the transporter room. "Riker to transporter room. Chief O'Brien, do you have a lock on the captain?"

"Aye, sir," O'Brien replied. "Ready when you are."

"Stand by." Riker blew out an uneasy breath. "All

right, Captain—I'm convinced. Geordi is on his way." As Riker spoke, La Forge was already rushing to the turbolift. "Which isn't to say I wouldn't *prefer* that you return to the *Enterprise,* sir."

"I am aware of your preference, Number One. But I believe I shall remain here. I think Captain Arit and I can put the time to good use."

"Lunchtime," Deana Troi called from the open shuttlecraft hatch.

Working at opposite sides of the cavern, Wesley and Gina picked up their tools and sample containers and converged on the ship. They climbed in, set their gear down and found Data and Troi in the aft cabin, waiting with small trays of heated rations.

"How would anyone *know* it's lunchtime?" Gina groused as she slid into a seat.

"It is twelve-hundred hours," Data said. "Is mid-day not the customary time for the mid-day meal? We are endeavoring to maintain a standard daily cycle."

Wesley shoveled a forkful of his food into his mouth. "I think Gina meant her question rhetorically, Commander."

"Don't tell me what I meant, Wesley! It's not day or night or *anything* down here and I—" She stopped abruptly and her eyes darted around the small cabin. "How come Kenny's not eating? What's he doing up there?" she said, nodding toward the cockpit.

Troi rose to her feet, sudden concern clouding her dark eyes. "I didn't know he was in the shuttle. I thought he was outside with you."

"He was," Wesley said. "But I thought he came back into the shuttle."

Data stood amidships, looking into the command cabin up front. "He is not here."

He turned to see Troi opening the hatch and jumping down. He followed her out, as did Wes and Gina. With flashlights in hand, they fanned out to search the corners of the cave and the openings of several tunnels converging on the main cavern, calling Kenny's name.

But only the echoes of their own voices replied.

They met back at the shuttle hatch. "It would appear that he is no longer in this immediate vicinity," Data said.

Wesley kicked the ground. *"Damn* him! I can't believe he did this."

"Cannot believe he did what, Wesley?" asked Data.

"Went looking for a way out of here."

"What?" Gina blurted with a disbelieving laugh. "Mr. 'I Don't Wanna Be in Caves'? Go wandering off by himself?"

Her face grim, Counselor Troi looked hard at Wesley. "What makes you think he went to search alone?"

"He *said* it, but I didn't think he meant it. *Damn* him—I never thought he'd *do* anything so stupid. *I* am *such* a jerk!"

"Ensign," Data said, "exactly what did Ken say?"

"He said the only way Gina would ever notice him was if he saved us singlehandedly."

Gina reacted with embarrassed amazement. "He said *what?"*

"I never thought he was serious," Wesley went on. "I thought it was just, y'know, guy talk."

"No, no, no," said Gina frantically. "You've *gotta* be wrong."

Wes sighed. "I wish I was."

The golden sparkle of energy alighted on the blossom of a tall flower swaying with thousands of others

127

in the breeze that blew gently across the hilltop. Ko wanted to be alone to think.

But her crimson adversary appeared in a twinkle directly above her. :**Your time is running out,**: said Mog.

:**It is not done yet,**: said Ko, who then disappeared instantly in an angry yellow flare.

Mog fluttered down to the flower tops, disappointed that he had not had more of an opportunity to taunt Ko about her inevitable failure. If only he could make her see the truth and avoid all this. How could Ko or anyone else possibly believe that other life existed beyond the Great Darkness? If such beliefs were not profane assaults on the Orthody, they would still be utterly preposterous fantasies. As the leader of those who opposed Ko's dangerous ideas, it was up to Mog to protect the World.

Perhaps he should never have agreed to give Ko even two cycles to try to communicate with these intruding things. Perhaps he should have just destroyed them as soon as he had discovered that Ko had snatched them from the darkness and brought them within the World. He could still change his mind and do just that.

But Mog had to remind himself to be patient. *Let Ko make her attempt. Let her discredit herself in front of all the Communion.* That was the best way to assure that no others would soon try so brazenly to contradict the Orthody.

Then Mog could destroy the intruders and be done with them.

Chapter Ten

ABOARD THE *Glin-Kale,* Arit paced the cramped office cubicle of her quarters while Picard sat at her desk and watched in silence. In theory, he had no trouble identifying with her conflict. He knew her driving motivation was the most basic instinct of all ship captains—to preserve their vessels and the people whose lives were entrusted to them.

He knew, too, that all captains also lived with an unspoken terror: having to face circumstances in which such salvation carried too high a price. Haunting every commander's nightmares, there were instances when his ship and those aboard her would have to be sacrificed in service to some higher principle or greater good. Since survival had to be the most ancient natural drive of living things, then overriding it had to be the most difficult task any sentient being would ever have to face.

And Picard had found himself in that most wrenching of positions on more than one occasion. He attributed the fact that he was still alive to contemplate the dilemma as much to good fortune as to his own skill and intelligence.

Theoretical empathy notwithstanding, however, Picard was unable to understand just why Arit had actually given serious thought to accepting the preventable destruction of the *Glin-Kale* and everyone aboard, rather than accepting help from the *Enterprise*. As long as the Tenirans refused to reveal the details of their plight, he could only guess. Their need to find a new home world was obviously urgent. Yet, something he could not see or grasp had nearly tipped the scales against basic survival.

Perhaps it was because he had no real idea of what it was like to be utterly homeless, adrift in the cosmos with no place to drop proverbial anchor. He recalled some history he'd read about the early days of travel outside the Terran solar system, when people from Earth were first able to journey so far from what had been the only home humanity had ever known. There'd been a movement to make "home" a vastly more expansive concept; star travelers were encouraged to think of home not as a country or region or town, but simply as Planet Earth (or Mars, or whatever station or moon they might have hailed from).

And it caught on, to some extent. But some people —Picard among them—resisted the loss of special identity that went with knowing you were from one specific place. Though he'd be the first to admit he'd spent most of his youth doing everything he could to get *away* from his own hometown, even his home planet, Picard had never felt rootless. His space travels had been by choice. And his ships had always served quite adequately as places to call "home" for as long as he served on them.

But, no matter how long he might be away, his real home would always be the house in the vineyards outside the sleepy French village of Labarre. Though he'd always made a point—perhaps too strenuously —to play the role of the contemporary man embracing the future and all it might offer, in sharp contrast to his adamantly archaic brother Robert, he had always been secretly grateful that someone had seen to it that the Picard homestead would remain a nearly unchanged oasis in time.

Picard had never felt that more keenly than on his most recent visit, just this past year, after recovering from his injuries sustained during the bloody encounter with the Borg. He hadn't been back to Labarre for almost twenty years . . . twenty years during which Robert had married Marie, and had their son, René. Twenty years during which Picard himself had risen to command the first of the mightiest starships known to humankind.

And yet, there amidst all the change, was a place that had not changed at all. A place that had nurtured generations of Picards for more than a century. An old stone house with wide-plank floorboards and well-worn rugs that still offered a singular comfort he knew he could not, and would not *ever,* find anywhere else. Not that he needed to *be* there all the time, or even often. But he needed to *know* it was there.

The feeling it gave him was an old-fashioned one, perhaps even quaint, especially in an era when people seemed to pick up and move from one planet to another with so little provocation. And, given a choice, it was a feeling Jean-Luc Picard would not trade for anything else he had ever known.

Perhaps the only way he could truly understand the

Teniran point of view would be to have all that taken away from him. In a way, then, it was a futile exercise to try to imagine how he would have reacted had he been in Arit's place. But he had always believed simple survival to be a priority that could open up quite a few possibilities. *Nonexistence, after all, is a bit of a dead end,* he thought, with a touch of gallows humor, and he was relieved that Arit had made the choice he believed he would have made.

"If there's a way to repair your engines, Commander La Forge will find it, Captain Arit," Picard said softly, doing his best to support her decision to accept help from the *Enterprise.*

"And what if there is no way to repair them? What happens then?" She stopped at an oval observation window and gazed out at the planet.

Picard wondered what that placid world meant to her. Did she see it as a last chance for redemption? Or did it simply represent the last in a long line of dashed hopes? And one nagging question would not go away: why in blazes was she so resistant to revealing anything about how her people had been forced to this terminus?

He got up and joined her at the window. "You know," he began cautiously, "we have very little in Federation data files about the Teniran Echelon."

"It's a big galaxy."

"That's true. But we both live in it, and like it or not, we are tangled in the same web of mysteries for the time being."

She turned and glared at him, real pain in her eyes. "The same web? I don't think so, Picard. What's your stake here—a tiny ship and a handful of people? *We're* fighting for our *existence.*"

"Which is what I have been saying all along," he

insisted. "If we understood your situation better, we might be able to offer some—"

"Our situation is ours, Picard," she said, cutting him off. But the fire was gone from her voice. "If your Federation files on us are meager, maybe that is the way we wanted it. And maybe we still do."

"But to what end, Arit? Why this shroud of secrecy around every detail of Teniran—"

The hiss of a door sliding open interrupted him in mid-sentence. He turned to see a Teniran child entering from an adjacent chamber, and he guessed by the resemblance that she was Arit's daughter.

"Keela," Arit scolded, "I told you to stay in your room."

"I know, Mother. But I thought Captain Picard might like some tea."

Picard couldn't help but notice the formal precision of the little girl's speech. Unlike some children who tried to imitate their elders, he believed Keela to be simply and naturally precocious. He smiled down at her. "We have not been officially introduced. I'm Captain Jean-Luc Picard."

"Yes, from the *Enterprise,*" Keela said. "I knew that."

"That's right. And how did you know that, Keela?"

Arit chuckled and Picard realized it was probably the first time he'd seen her smile. "My daughter seems to know most of what's going on here on the *Glin-Kale.*"

"Well, it is a pleasure to meet you, Keela."

"You have a very pretty ship, Captain," the little girl said.

"Thank you very much."

"I would very much like to see it. Do you think that would be possible?"

Picard glanced at her mother, then back at Keela. "It might be—though I suppose that is up to your mother. We'll see."

Arit cleared her throat. "You offered the captain tea. Don't you think you should set about making it?"

Keela's head tilted in a gesture of exasperation so adult it nearly made Picard laugh. "It's already made, Mother. I'll go get it." She turned and went back to the other room.

"Your daughter seems to be a very self-possessed young lady."

"That she is," Arit said with a sigh of maternal resignation. "Do you have children, Picard?"

"Uhh, no—no, I don't," he said with a self-conscious flicker in his eyes. "Why do you ask?"

"No particular reason. Just that adults don't always know quite what to make of Keela, and you seem quite comfortable with her."

"A recently developed skill, I assure you. I'd never had much exposure to young people—until I took command of the *Enterprise*. We have families aboard. I suppose that four years of chance encounters with children on my ship have actually taught me something," he said, a self-deprecating smile playing across his lips.

A moment later, Keela returned, carefully balancing a tray carrying three ceramic cups and the teapot. As she reached the desk, Picard's communicator chirped and they heard Geordi's voice.

"La Forge to Captain Picard."

"Picard here. Have you completed your evaluation, Commander?"

"Yes, sir. We managed to stabilize the magnetic containment fields in their power core, so there's no immediate danger of destruction. But I've gotta tell you, these engines are being held together with spit and chewing gum."

"The Teniran phrase," said Picard, "is 'threads and wishes,' I believe."

"Okay," Geordi said ruefully, "then they're hanging by a thread."

"And will you be able to provide the stitch in time, so to speak?"

"I think so, sir. But I can't say they'll be as good as new. If these engines were cats, they'd be on their ninth life."

"But you *can* restore them to operating condition?"

"I'd say eighty-percent probability, sir. And if we do get 'em up and running, then I'd urge the Tenirans—in no uncertain terms—to head for the nearest fully equipped repair base for a total overhaul. Other than that, we're ready to get started. Awaiting your orders."

"Make it so, Mr. La Forge." He paused. "And, excellent work."

"Thanks, Captain, but I think I'd hold the applause until we actually get things fixed down here."

"Hey . . . Gina . . ."

At the tentative sound of Wesley Crusher's voice, she looked up from the cave floor where she'd been sitting alongside the shuttlecraft, leaning back against the engine nacelle. She held her small drawing pad in her lap and Wes could see she'd been sketching a charcoal of their cavern prison, artwork as bleak as her mood. "Mind if I sit down?" he asked.

She shrugged. "If you want to sit on cold, damp rock, be my guest. Has Data come back yet?"

Wes shook his head. "At least that means he hasn't given up."

"It also means he hasn't found Kenny yet." She

gnawed on her lower lip and stared at the ground. "Data should've let me go with him."

"What difference would it make for two people to cover the same ground as he can by himself?"

"What they *really* should've done is let me go off and search by myself. Then we could've covered twice as much tunnel in the same amount of time."

"You *knew* they wouldn't let you go alone. Just what we need—two kids lost in this maze of tunnels."

She gave him a belligerent glare. "Me? Get lost in a cave? In what century?"

"That's not the point," Wesley said gently.

"Oh, yeah?" she flared. "Then what *is* the point?"

He started to say something, then swallowed it, finishing up with a helpless shrug. "I . . . I don't know, Gina."

"Ohhh, Wesley," she moaned, her shoulders slumping. "I had no idea he liked me. Do you really think he did this to impress me? I can't believe *anybody* would do anything that dumb . . . and I can't believe how guilty *I'm* gonna feel for the rest of my life if anything happens to him."

"You shouldn't feel guilty. It's not your fault."

Gina's head snapped up and she frowned at him. "You're right. I *shouldn't* feel guilty. *I* didn't make him do this. I didn't twist his arm and say 'Go be a hero!' Did I say that? Did I even *hint* at anything like that? *Damn right, I didn't!*"

She waited for Wesley to react to her anger, and she wanted him to tell her over and over how it wasn't her fault, no matter what happened. Instead, he seemed distracted by something over her shoulder, up in a deep, dark corner of the cavern. She turned to find out what could be more important than making her feel better.

There it was—a tiny golden spark, glittering in the gloom. They both rose slowly to their feet and took a couple of hesitant steps toward it. The sparkle edged toward them, then stopped and hovered. Gina flipped to a fresh page in her pad and began sketching furiously. She and Wesley spoke in hushed voices.

"Wes, what do you think it is? An insect, maybe? Like a fire-fly or something?"

"I have no idea . . . but I'd love to find out." He backed off toward the shuttle. "Keep an eye on it—I'm going to get a tricorder."

Sidling over to the shuttle so he wouldn't have to turn his back completely, he rapped gently on the hull next to the open hatch. "Deanna," he called in a loud whisper, "hand me a tricorder."

Counselor Troi appeared and handed the device down to him. "Wesley, is something wrong?"

"No. There's this . . . this *sparkle* that just appeared and I wanted to take some . . ." He looked away from Gina and toward Troi for just an instant and when he looked back, he saw that Gina had stopped drawing and just stood there, her shoulders slouched in disappointment. ". . . some readings. Damn!"

Wes rushed back over to her, with Troi trailing behind.

"Gina, what happened to it?" he asked.

"It just sort of . . . winked out."

Troi stepped around to face them. "What winked out?"

Gina handed her the sketchpad and Troi gazed at the hasty drawing. Wesley had used the word *sparkle*, and that's exactly what Gina had drawn.

Troi returned the pad. "What did it do?"

"Nothing much," said Wesley.

"It just popped in," Gina added, "hung there for a minute like a Christmas star, and then it was gone."

Troi's dark eyes scanned the cavern as she concentrated all her empathic powers, trying to sense even the slightest presence of life-energy. Wesley and Gina watched her silently. After a few moments, she shook her head. "I'm not getting anything."

"If it comes back," Wesley said, "maybe we'll get a better chance to study it."

"Wes, weren't you working on the communications system?" asked Gina.

"Yes, and I think I'm finally making some progress."

"Then why don't you and Counselor Troi work on that, and I'll stay outside the shuttle and keep watch for any more sparkly things."

Wes nodded. "Okay. That sounds like a good idea."

"Just make sure you stay close to the shuttle," Troi said firmly. "Don't wander off."

"I won't . . . I'll be right around the ship."

Gina waited until they'd gone back inside, leaving her alone. Then she circled the shuttlecraft, pivoting slowly, searching. Finally satisfied that there weren't any of the little glittering light points present, she tiptoed directly to one of the tunnels leading away from the main cavern and disappeared into the darkness.

For the next hour or so, Counselor Troi busied herself in the *Onizuka*'s aft cabin with updates on her evaluations of the young away-team members, while Wesley struggled under the cockpit consoles to restore some minimal function to the shuttle's severely damaged communications system.

But Troi knew she was just filling time. These evaluations were not exactly a high priority. Once they made it back to the *Enterprise,* she'd have plenty of opportunity to complete these file entries. And if they wound up stranded here, then the evaluations would obviously be of no consequence.

She thought of the *Enterprise,* and all the efforts that she knew were being expended to find the missing shuttlecraft and its crew. Troi had witnessed enough search missions to know how resourceful her shipmates could be when the lives of colleagues hung in the balance. They would be doing everything possible to retrieve the away team, and quite likely delving into the impossible as well.

But Deanna also knew all too well that even the best efforts did not always yield the desired results. And at the same time as she tried to concentrate on the probability that they would be rescued, she knew she also had to prepare herself for the *possibility* that they would not.

Up front, as Wesley rerouted surviving circuitry inside the communications module, he considered the concept of *being missing. We're not missing,* he mused. *We know where we are . . . but if the* Enterprise *doesn't find us, and we survive this, then we'll be marooned here. To them, we'll be missing forever, even though we're still alive.* He did not like that eerie idea at all.

The side hatch slid open and both Wesley and Deanna looked up as Data climbed in. Alone.

Troi's lips thinned to a grim line. "You didn't find him." It was a statement, not a question.

"No, I did not," Data said in a voice that made it hard to believe this android did not have genuine human feelings.

Wes sat on the cockpit deck, his head bowed. "I guess Gina is pretty depressed, huh?"

Data cocked his head questioningly. "Depressed about what, Wesley?"

"About your not finding Kenny."

"But how would she know? I did not tell her."

"You mean she didn't meet you outside the shuttle when you got back?" Wes asked, bewildered by Data's statement.

"No, she did not. I assumed that she was in the shuttle with you, but I see that is not the case."

"But we left her outside to keep watch," Troi began.

"She did it," Wesley muttered as he stood, shaking his head in anger and frustration. "I don't believe this—she really did it."

"Did what, Wesley?" Data asked.

Troi knew. "She went to look for Ken, didn't she?"

Wes answered with a wordless nod and a hollow look in his eyes. "She wanted to go search when you did, Commander," he finally said to Data. "She blamed herself for Kenny's running off—she really wanted to help find him."

"An intriguingly human reaction," Data said, "and one which adds a distinct complication to our predicament . . . we must now find both of them in addition to finding a way out of this place."

Chapter Eleven

THE *GLIN-KALE* COASTED AROUND Domarus Four in its powerless orbit while Geordi La Forge and his engineering team continued their engine resuscitation work. Knowing how he'd feel if the situation had been reversed, Geordi had felt more than a little uncomfortable invading somebody else's engine room. The Teniran chief engineer, Naladi, had greeted the *Enterprise* team of four with open suspicion when they'd first come aboard. But orders were orders, and the word from Captain Arit on the bridge had been precise—*let them work.*

Naladi had actually shooed most of his own staff out of the engine bay, as if he wanted as few witnesses to his shame as possible. But Geordi had made every effort to ask questions of the Tenirans, and to brief them every step of the way, so they not only knew what was being done but also felt a part of the process. He was banking on all the tinkering to bring about a phenomenon he'd seen often enough before—a sort of universal brotherhood of engineers.

His faith paid off. Within an hour, Geordi and Naladi found themselves working side by side.

Meanwhile, Picard and Captain Arit had returned to the bridge to find First Officer Jevlin and the Teniran command crew mesmerized by a sight both captains had come to be wary of—the viewscreen image of uncountable ribbons of color doing a frenzied dance just off the *Glin-Kale*'s bow. The light from the tumble of colors flickered through the entire bridge.

Despite the unsettling experiences he'd already had, Picard found himself drawn toward the viewer. "Absolutely fascinating," he murmured.

"I could do with somewhat less fascination in my life," Arit said dryly as she stopped a pace behind Picard.

He turned back toward her. "Aren't you the least bit curious about what it might mean?"

"Curiosity is a luxury I can't really afford right now, Picard."

He sensed a touch of envy in her voice, as if she wished she could feel what he did. "Then you've got more self-control than I do. Ever since childhood, I have found it very, very difficult to resist the lure of a riddle or a puzzle, the challenge to know the unknown." The dancing colors from outside the ship reflected in his eyes.

"Unfortunately, the unknown is all too often unwelcome," Arit pointed out, tension etched into taut lines around her mouth.

"Then why explore?"

"Even in the best of times, we Tenirans have never really been explorers. And since these are far from the best of times for us, now we just want a safe place to call home."

The exit hatch creaked and opened . . . halfway. Geordi and his three propulsion experts—two women and a man—squeezed through and came onto the bridge.

"I could try fixing that," La Forge offered, thumbing back at the reluctant hatch.

"We'll deal with it," Jevlin said curtly.

Picard moved over to intercede. "Your report, Commander La Forge?"

"Well, sir, we did the best we could. You've got a crack engineering team down there, Captain Arit. Between their familiarity with your propulsion systems and our technology, we managed to get things patched together. She won't set any speed or endurance records, but she'll get where you're going—as long as you're not going too far."

"Thank you, Commander La Forge," Arit said.

"You're more than welcome, Captain."

Arit turned to Picard. "Then you'll be leaving now, Picard," she said, her tone brusque.

He had not expected to be discharged quite so hastily and his eyebrows hitched up in surprise. "Actually, I had hoped our assistance might establish a bit more trust between us."

Jevlin shouldered his way into the exchange. "I told you, Cap'n Arit—nothing comes for free."

"With all due respect, you are wrong," Picard said. "I said there would be no strings tied to our offer of help and I meant it. I just hoped you might be willing to tell us more about the Teniran people, and the circumstances that brought you to Domarus Four."

"With all due respect, Picard," Arit said with a mocking chill in her voice, "if we wish to keep our past confidential, that is our business. We have no obligation to satisfy your curiosity."

"That's right," the Teniran first officer added, thumping his walking stick on the deck for emphasis. "Just leave us to our planet."

Picard's jaw tightened. This was not going at all the way he had envisioned. He thought they'd made some real progress during the past couple of hours, but perhaps he'd only seen what he'd wanted to see. The Tenirans obviously did not see things as he did.

"Then we are back to our unresolved conflict," he said evenly, his tone and phrasing expressing quiet insistence—he was not going to back down. "We still have not ascertained the fate of our missing shuttlecraft, and this is not your planet for the taking. We have all witnessed the same evidence suggesting that Domarus may harbor sentient life. For your own safety, if for no other reason, I should think you would want to cooperate with us in figuring out whether or not Domarus is inhabited by—"

"By those colored energy patterns?" Jevlin said dismissively. "They're not any evidence of anything —and you've got no authority to order *us* around. Now unless you want yourselves to be considered prisoners—"

Arit cut her first officer off with an imperious wave of her hand. "Jevlin has a nasty temper at times, Captain Picard," she said, intentionally calm now. "You are, of course, free to go, with our thanks. But, if necessary, we will fight for our right to settle here."

"Captain Arit, I do not believe combat to be the solution to your dilemma . . . and I don't think you do, either. There are other alternatives."

"For *you,* Picard, there may be alternatives—not for us. Here is where we choose to stay, and let me be clear about this: after all we've been through, we *are*

144

willing to die for that choice. If the *Enterprise* uses force to try and stop us—"

"We will not," Picard said. "But if there *are* advanced life forms on Domarus, they may perceive you as invaders. *They* may use force—in ways we cannot even begin to imagine."

"If that's the case, then it *will* end here after all, Picard."

"Arit, I cannot believe—"

Before Picard could finish, before anyone could react, he and Arit were suddenly enveloped in a rush of swirling colors. An instant later, the colors vanished from the bridge as abruptly as they'd appeared, and the two captains vanished with them.

"Shields up!" Jevlin shouted. "Defensive priority!"

On the *Enterprise* bridge, Lieutenant Worf growled deep in his throat.

"What is it, Mr. Worf?" said Riker from the command seat, turning to face the Klingon security chief.

Worf's brow ridges deepened into a glower. "The Teniran ship has just raised its shields, sir."

"What the hell?" Riker said, eyes narrowing as he stood. "Raise our shields and open a channel to the *Glin-Kale.*"

"Shields up—channel open, Commander."

Riker took two strides toward the viewscreen and planted his feet in a belligerent stance. *"Enterprise* to *Glin-Kale.* This is Commander Riker. You have violated our truce accord by raising your shields. Why?"

First Officer Jevlin appeared on screen, standing in the center of his bridge. The old Teniran's eyes flicked from side to side, as if trying to keep track of chaos around him, betraying the agitation he struggled to banish from his voice. "We have our reasons," he answered in a lame attempt at defiance.

Riker could see Geordi and his trio of engineers waiting just behind Jevlin, apparently unharmed and unrestricted. *But where is the captain? Dammit—I knew I shouldn't have let him stay over there.* "Let me speak to Captain Picard."

"That is not possible, Commander. Let me speak to Captain Arit."

Riker's eyes narrowed. "We don't have your captain."

"Then they're both gone, gods know where."

"Geordi—"

La Forge stepped forward. "Here, Commander."

"Is he telling the truth?"

"I'm afraid so, sir. Same deal—that multicolored energy pattern again."

"And until Captain Arit is returned to this ship," Jevlin said harshly, "your engineers will stay right here in our custody. *Glin-Kale* out."

Seconds after Jevlin's determined face faded from the viewscreen, the now-familiar whorls of color and their collateral sounds filled the heart of the *Enterprise* bridge. Worf leaped over the railing, intent on protecting Riker more effectively than he'd been able to protect his captain a day ago.

But this time, the enigmatic energy phenomenon hadn't come to abduct anyone. Instead, it deposited Picard and Arit near the big viewscreen, then promptly dissolved.

Picard found he was getting accustomed to these precipitous changes of venue, and he recovered his balance quickly, tugged at the hem of his tunic to straighten it, and acknowledged the gapes of his stunned bridge crew with an unruffled nod of greeting.

Then he turned to the shaken Teniran commander. "Captain Arit—welcome to the *Enterprise.*"

For as far back as she could remember in her sixteen years, Gina Pace had never feared the unknowns lurking around the next corner or hunkered in the dark shadows just beyond her vision. As a child, she had never given this lack of fear much thought—just followed her natural curiosity to know and see what she hadn't seen before.

But now, as she neared adulthood, new perspectives presented themselves. And she would occasionally find herself wondering why some people—like Kenny Kolker, for instance—approached the unknown so differently from the way she did, freighted with dreads and anxieties that for some reason simply didn't intrude on her life. Not that the wondering had changed her. She still followed her nose, more or less, with unwavering faith that whatever waited around the next bend would be worth the journey—and would not kill her.

And for the present, she believed Kenny would be around the next bend in the maze of Domaran caves and tunnels. Or around the bend after that. She *would* find him.

She followed a tunnel that narrowed to the point where she had to crouch and scuttle to keep moving forward. The pool of light from her lantern cut the gloom and revealed a fork just ahead. She chose the left branch and was pleased to find that it opened up in both width and height, permitting her to stand. *A good omen maybe . . . ?*

Or maybe not. She panned her light beam ahead and saw that the tunnel dead-ended, and—

"There's no way out this way," said a voice in the

darkness, making her heart jump with reflexive fright. "Believe me."

Kenny's voice!

She swept her flashlight beam across the tunnel and found him against the cave wall, huddled on a flat outcropping of rock, the fingers of one hand fanned out before his face as he tried to block out the glare of her light.

"Sorry," she said, pointing it up like a torch.

"That's better." He flicked his own light on and together they provided softer illumination for the small cul de sac. "How did you find me?"

Gina shrugged. "I just did, that's all. Are you okay?"

"Yeah, I guess so. I'm feeling a little hungry. A little tired." His expression betrayed his inner uncertainty. "A little stupid. Other than that, okay."

She came closer to him, shaking her head. "What in the whole wide universe possessed you to pull a stunt like this?"

"It wasn't a stunt," he protested. But the reality of the situation drained the fight out of him. "I just thought . . . I might find a way out."

"Oh," she said neutrally. "Did you really do this to impress me?"

"No!" he bleated indignantly, then sighed and hung his head. "And if I did, the plan sure backfired."

"Maybe it did . . . maybe it didn't."

He glanced at her from beneath his embarrassed frown. "What do you mean? I blew it. I disregarded orders—and on top of that, I got lost. How much more could I have screwed up?"

"Let me give that some thought. Not that I'm defending what you did or your obvious lack of success."

"Great . . . kick me while I'm down."

"I'm just saying that what you did was kind of, well . . . sweet. Stupid . . . but sweet."

"Yeah?" he said, brightening.

"Yeah." She managed a shy smile, then extended her hand and pulled him to his feet. "We better get back. I'm sure they're having a fit looking for me by now, not to mention you."

Gina's hidden meaning dawned on him. "Huh? You mean, they don't know you went looking for me? *You* did the same thing *I* did?"

The comparison obviously offended her. "The same as you did? Not exactly. After all, I *did* find you—and I'm not lost. C'mon."

"Maybe I *should* return to the *Glin-Kale*, Jevlin . . . maybe you're right. But I'm not ready to come back. Not yet."

Captain Arit leaned across the conference-room table, looking at the disapproving image of her first officer on the table-top viewscreen. Picard, Riker and Dr. Crusher sat there, too, waiting.

"How do I know you're not a prisoner, Cap'n?"

"I'm not a prisoner, any more than Picard was on our ship. But we've got things to discuss, and now is the time to do it."

"But, Cap'n, our people are ready to take this Domarus Four and make it home."

"Not without my authorization . . . and I am no longer sure that Domarus is the place for us, Jevlin."

The Teniran first officer jumped to his feet and pounded his walking stick on the deck. "Don't tell me you're going along with Picard's fantasy tales about intelligent life down on the planet."

"Intelligent life? Who knows. But *something* unexplained is going on down there, and only a fool would send her people down to settle a place that could pose grave dangers. I may be a lot of things, Jevlin . . . but I am not ready to answer to 'fool.'"

She saw her old friend slump back into the *Glin-Kale*'s command seat, subservient for the moment. "I suppose you'll be wanting me to release these engineers then."

"I think Captain Picard would like them back, yes. If it's not too much trouble for you, Jevlin," Arit said tartly.

"Our shields are being lowered now, Cap'n. They're free to go."

Riker activated his insignia communicator. "Riker to transporter room."

"O'Brien here, sir," came the intercom reply.

"Lock onto Geordi's team and beam them back."

"They're as good as here, Commander. O'Brien out."

Picard rested his clasped hands on the table. "Thank you, Captain. And I am pleased that you chose to stay and discuss the situation. The fate of your people rests in your hands—I do believe you've made the correct choice."

Arit cocked a skeptical eyebrow. "That remains to be seen."

Chapter Twelve

"I'VE NEVER SEEN anything like this network of tunnels," Gina said as she led Ken back through the underground labyrinth. "It's hard to believe all this formed naturally."

"You know, I was wondering about that. Not that I have so much subterranean experience, but there seemed to be almost a system here—though I couldn't even begin to make any sense out of it. That's why I wasn't *too* nervous when I realized I was lost."

"You mean, you figured if there really *is* a system at work here, somebody would find you?"

"Pretty much."

Gina gave him a searching look. "So you weren't scared out here by yourself?"

"Maybe a little, at first. But it wasn't as bad as I thought it would be. It was actually kind of peaceful, in a way. I got to thinking, wondering . . . if maybe death is something like this."

As they bent down to crawl through a narrow

stretch of the passage, she glanced at him quizzically. "You lost me on that one."

"I mean, maybe death is like walking down a tunnel that gets more and more narrow . . . kind of cool and dark, and quiet and private."

"But what about all those near-death or back-from-the-dead experiences people tell about—there's always a bright light at the end of the tunnel. The only bright light here was this—" She briefly flashed her light in his eyes. "So what did you find at the end?"

"Nothing. I mean, maybe it's like I'm still alive, so I never got to the end. Or maybe there *isn't* any end." He was quiet for a moment. "Oh, hell, I don't know."

"No," Gina teased, "they say hell would have fire and brimstone."

They emerged from the narrow confines of a branch tunnel. Gina's calm confident stride left no doubts that she knew exactly where they were headed. "You know, you left your poetry notebook out," she said.

"I did?"

"Aha! So it *was* a poem you were writing the other day."

"So?" His tone was plainly defensive.

"So, nothing."

"Did you read any of it?" he asked, steeling himself for a barrage of ridicule.

"No. I found it in the cockpit." She paused. "And I put it away with the rest of your stuff."

Now Kenny seemed insulted. "You mean you *didn't* read it? Why not?"

"You seemed to want to keep it private. So I respected that. Not that I wasn't curious . . . I mean, you don't seem like the poetry-writing type," she said as they sidestepped a pool a few inches deep, fed by water that trickled down the tunnel wall and collected in a shallow depression.

"Well, I wasn't. But I once did a computer project analyzing the symmetry of rhymes."

Gina seemed to regard that to be a tenuous link at best. "And that's how you started writing poems?"

"Yeah. What's so strange about that? Don't you think there's a lot of art in science and science in art?"

"I don't know. I never really thought about it that way." She was a little surprised to hear something that thought provoking out of Kenny. *Maybe there's more to him than I thought* . . . "Tell me something."

"What?"

"Why don't you want anyone to know you write poetry?"

"I don't know," he said with a short shrug. "You said it yourself—people just don't look at me and think 'Ah, he's a *poet!*'"

"Y'know, I've liked to draw and paint ever since I can remember. But when I was little, I'd do it in secret, in my room with the door shut. When I started school, I wouldn't do art when all the other kids did."

"Really?"

"Mm-hmm. No matter how my teacher tried, she just couldn't get me to draw in class. I was one stubborn little kid, and I just didn't want anyone to see my stuff."

Ken gave her a quizzical look. "Why not?"

"I don't really know. For some reason, I just got it in my head that these drawings were *mine,* something private. Not something to be shared."

"What made you change your mind?"

Gina smiled. "My grandma. She found one of my paintings. It was a picture of the mountains outside our town. You know how other people put their kids' art up in the kitchen or someplace like that?"

"Yeah."

"Well, my grandma had this painting framed in this gorgeous antique wooden frame . . . and she made a big deal of telling me that she loved the painting so much that she was going to hang it in her bedroom, next to her bed, so it would be the last thing she'd see when she went to sleep at night, and the first thing she'd see when she got up in the morning. And she made me promise to show all my pictures to her. And that's when I knew that whatever else I did, I'd always want to be an artist."

"That's a nice story, Gina."

"Yeah." She looked him straight in the eye. "If people don't see you as a poet, maybe that's because you won't let them. Maybe you should change that."

"Picard, you said yourself that you've detected nothing down there that could be called sentient life," Arit insisted as she paced around the curved table in the *Enterprise* conference room, circling behind the captain, Riker and Dr. Crusher.

Picard peered calmly over his steepled fingers. "Not conclusively, perhaps. But the indirect evidence does seem to point in that direction. Would you disagree with that?"

Arit stopped and gripped the headrest of her chair. "All I will agree to is that *some* force we don't understand appears to be present on the planet and in the orbital vicinity of Domarus. Nothing more, nothing less."

"With all due respect, Captain Arit," said Riker, "you sound like a lawyer."

She fixed Riker with a measured look. "Maybe

that's because I have to defend my people's right to settle on an uninhabited planet that seems to belong to no one, and that no one but *you* seems to care about."

Picard shook his head. "Captain, no one is prosecuting you. And this contentiousness is getting us nowhere—" The rolling beep of the intercom interrupted him, followed by Engineer La Forge's voice over the speaker.

"La Forge to Captain Picard."

"Picard here. Have you completed that cumulative evaluation of our sensor readings?"

"That's why I'm calling, Captain. We'll need maybe another hour to get it together."

Picard scowled. "I thought you expected to be done by now."

"Well, we would've been—but sensors just started picking up a big jump in energy cycling from Domarus."

"Energy cycling?" Arit repeated, not sure what Geordi meant.

"Right," Geordi said. "Production *and* utilization."

"Mr. La Forge," Picard said, "do you have any idea what might be going on down there?"

"Not yet, sir. But we're doing our best to figure it out."

"Very well. Report to the conference lounge as soon as you are ready. Picard out." He faced Arit, who had finally sat back down. "Captain, let's cut to the heart of the matter. I want my missing shuttle and crew members back—and you need a home for your people. If I did not believe we could achieve both, I would not have invited you to remain on the *Enterprise.*"

"And I wouldn't have accepted if *I* didn't also believe we could both get what we want."

"Well, then, this sounds like a promising start."

"A start," Arit said wearily as she tried to rub the fatigue from her eyes. "That's all we're seeking, Picard—a place for a fresh start."

Beverly stared at the Teniran commander. "Then why won't you let us help you find that place?"

"It is not—" Arit began, then stopped, rubbing one lower fang against her upper lip as she sighed in frustration. "It is not an easy thing for us to reveal our vulnerabilities. You would understand if you knew our recent history."

"How can we know your recent history," Beverly said, not without compassion, "if you won't tell us?"

"And, not to be insulting, Captain Arit," Riker said, "but we already know your vulnerabilities. We know the condition of your ship."

"Perhaps you do, Commander Riker. But none of that changes the core of our dispute—you remain opposed to our goal."

"On the contrary," Picard said with a raised finger. "We want to avoid any actions around Domarus that may hinder the retrieval of our missing shuttle and crew members, of course. But beyond that, our opposition is based solely on one point—the need to be certain that no sentient life forms already exist on Domarus Four. Now, you were absolutely correct when you said you have every right to keep your past confidential—"

Arit cut him off, shaking her head as if trying to clear it. "And Commander Riker was right—you already know our weakness. And I can't ignore the fact that you have not taken advantage of that knowledge." She allowed herself an ironic chuckle. "Even if you *were* hostile, we don't exactly have anything you could possibly want. It's just dawned on me how liberating it is to realize you've got nothing left to defend."

Arit took a deep breath, paused at her internal crossroads, then chose her direction. "You were also correct, Captain Picard, when you said that we've traveled a hard road."

"Are you ready to tell us about it?"

"Yes, I suppose I am," she said with a nod, and she seemed relieved to be sharing the burden at last. "Unpredictable changes in our sun caused catastrophic climate changes that turned our farmlands to desert, brought on terrible rains that flooded the lowlands, whipped up devastating storms everywhere. Nothing could be done. Our scientists tried. The only fortunate aspect of the whole disaster was that we did have enough time to plan an evacuation of most of our people before Tenira became totally uninhabitable."

"How large a population?" Crusher asked.

"Not large compared to many planets—about ten million."

"That is small," said Riker.

"That's because our land masses are small compared to a lot of worlds, so we had to develop strict population control and balance long ago."

Picard frowned. "Ten million may constitute a small population, but it is a sizable evacuation. Where were you going to go with ten million people?"

"Well, we were ready to split up and live wherever we could, hoping someday we could reassemble all our people—or at least their descendants—on one world. But then one of our trading partners, Ziakk, offered us a planet in their star system. A savage, untamed world—but habitable for people willing to put in a lot of hard work."

"They offered it to you, just like that?" Dr. Crusher asked.

"So it seemed at the time. They wanted this planet developed, but they said they did not have enough Ziakkans willing to make the kind of sacrifices required of pioneers."

Riker sipped a steaming cup of coffee. "But you took it?"

"There's an old Teniran proverb, Commander Riker: 'the starving beast can't be too picky about whose garbage he eats.' That's a fair description of our situation. The Ziakkan offer looked like the answer to our prayers—a place all Tenirans could be together."

"But something obviously went wrong," Picard said.

"Yes it did, Captain. It turned out the Ziakkans didn't want partners, they wanted *slaves*. Tenirans are *not* slaves," Arit said with fierce pride. But she turned pensive again as she recalled the events that followed. "We declared our independence—and they declared war. Biological war. We had no time or resources to build adequate defenses . . . within six months, most of our people were dead. Including my husband."

"Attempted genocide," Crusher said in a horrified whisper.

"Very nearly successful. Those of us who survived realized we couldn't win, so we fled. The *Glin-Kale* and her five thousand passengers are all that is left."

Beverly blanched as she tried to grasp the magnitude of the Tenirans' loss. "Five thousand left out of ten million? That's unbelievable, an unbelievable tragedy."

"But true. Now perhaps you can all understand why Domarus is so important to us."

After an awkward silence, Picard exhaled a contemplative breath and spoke softly. "The Federation will help you find a home, Captain. If not here, somewhere else. But I will offer you a promise: the Teniran people will not be doomed to wander."

"Gina, I thought you said we should hurry back to the ship."

"Oh, come on, Kenny—I want you to see this. It's not like it's out of our way."

Gina and Kenny were struggling to keep their footing as they made their way up through a steeply inclined section of the tunnels. As Kenny was about to press his argument against any detour, however slight, his right boot skidded on some loose pebbles and he flung a hand out to grab the cave wall for support.

"Not that I've got any choice other than following you," he groused.

She gave him a smile of supremacy. "That's right."

"So what's so special that I *have* to see it?"

"You'll see."

He cocked his ear. "Sounds like a waterfall."

They reached the trail's crest, then followed the gentle downhill slope. The echo of cascading water grew louder, approaching a roar. Without warning, Gina stopped and Kenny bumped into her.

"Kenny—be careful—" she shouted over the thunder of the water.

As she warned him, she tipped her flashlight down, revealing that the trail ended in a ledge no more than a meter ahead of them. Kenny gasped when he saw how close they'd come to tumbling over the rim. Then, when she widened her beam and fanned it out in the darkness, he simply gaped in wonder.

The overlook opened onto a towering cathedral of rough rock, streaked with glimmering veins of minerals, reds and golds and greens and blues, in patterns of such astonishing geometry they almost *had* to have been planned. If the grotto had a ceiling, it was lost in the darkness hundreds of feet above them, far beyond the range of their searchlights. A silver ribbon of water tumbled over a similar ledge across the cavern, twenty meters away from where they stood, and plunged into an abyss so deep they couldn't see the bottom.

"So," she yelled, "what do you think of my discovery? Pretty incredible, huh?" With more than a little glee, she watched as Kenny blinked in amazement several times before he could answer. And she took pleasure from the fact he seemed to have lost all his fear of being underground. He actually seemed as awestruck as she had been when she found this place.

"This is . . . wow!" he finally managed to say.

Gina snickered. "You're so articulate when you're astounded." Then she sighed. Never in her life had she seen anything like some of the wonders hidden deep inside this enigmatic world; it was just plain frustrating that she did not have the time to explore them properly. If she could summon up the nerve, she planned to ask Captain Picard for a return trip to Domarus—that is, if they ever got *off* Domarus. "I wish I at least had an hour to do a painting of all this."

"But we don't. We'd better get going." He paused and squinted into the darkness at something just above the lip of the waterfall. "What are those things up there?"

"What are what things up where?"

He pointed and she followed his finger. Then she

saw them too—a pair of slowly twirling sparks of fire, one golden, the other a brilliant ice-blue, splinters of brightness pinwheeling in place above the narrow stream just before the falls. She immediately rose up on her toes with excitement. "Oooh, I don't believe this! Two of them!"

"Two of what? Have you seen these things before?"

"Yeah—I mean, at least it *looks* like what Wesley and I saw near the shuttle. But we only saw one of them."

"One of *what?* What *are* they?"

"I have no idea," Gina called as she advanced right to the edge of the path, wishing she could get closer. "The one we saw disappeared before we had a chance to scan it with the tricorder."

"Whatever they may be, they are most intriguing," a new voice said from behind them—Data's voice, making them both jump.

"Commander!" Gina gasped, clutching her chest and trying to calm her breathing. "If you weren't an android, I'd think you were really ticked off at us."

"If I were not an android," he said, "I would be. Your unauthorized excursions will not enhance your performance evaluations for this mission."

Kenny, who had been rendered speechless by Data's surprise arrival, found his voice and pointed across the cavern. "Hey—look what they're doing."

Data and Gina aimed their lights over just as the sparkles seemed to stall. But their stillness only lasted for a few seconds. Then the tiny energy motes burst into a frenzied dance that quickly became too rapid for the human eye to follow in detail. In their wake, they threw off streamers of colors that coalesced into a multihued helix, spinning and whirling and caroming off the cave-cathedral's walls, seeming ever on the verge of changing, yet always holding its fundamental intertwined shape. A second helix formed, then another and another, and others after that.

Ken and Gina, and even Data, stood transfixed by the luminous energy spirals as they spawned and linked, finally forming a vibrant grid that seemed *alive* as it filled the entire core of the grotto and enveloped the walls—yet leaving a buffer around the three starship visitors. Starting at the low threshold of their hearing, a chorus of clinks and jangles rose in both pitch and intensity, quickly drowning out the roaring waterfall and forcing Ken and Gina to cover their ears.

Their android chaperon continued to listen and observe—Gina knew his sensory circuitry could simply compensate for the excessive input, probably without limit. She wished she could do the same.

Simultaneous with the explosion of sound, the energy helixes blazed to a super-white brightness too painful for humans to watch. But Gina struggled to keep her eyes open against the overwhelming radiance because of what she *thought* she saw behind it— *impossible.*

The walls of the grotto—*solid rock*—seemed to be running, transfiguring like molten ore. But she felt no heat at all. *What's happening here?*

She surrendered to the bright light, clamping her eyes shut, ducking her head and burying her face in her arms as she turned away and fell to her knees, ending up curled into a protective ball.

After an interval that seemed like hours but was really only a matter of five seconds, Gina became aware that the sunburst had faded. She sat up and tried to look, but her eyes were slow to adjust after the blinding brightness she'd tried in vain to witness moments before. Her heart raced with impatience as she blinked deeply, waiting for a return of visual clarity. She felt Kenny next to her.

"Are you okay?" he said, a quaver in his voice.

"Yeah, I guess so. How about you?"

"I'm all right, I guess. Are your eyes okay?"

"Getting there." As she spoke, it dawned on her that she wasn't shouting. The waterfall thunder that had filled the grotto was gone, replaced by stunning, crystalline silence. There was no sound at all other than their breathing. *What is going on here?!*

She felt Data's cool strong grip on her arm as he helped her to her feet. He had picked up her flashlight and added that beam to his own, one in each hand, illuminating as much of the cavern as he could.

Gina's eyes finally accustomed themselves to the dimmer light, and she looked around. With a wide-eyed shiver, she discovered that the interior of the cavern had *changed*. The slope of the walls, the patterns of the mineral veins, it was all different.

And the waterfall really was gone—*without the slightest remaining hint that it had ever been there.*

Ko's twirling slowed perceptibly as the realization set in: the live things still did not comprehend. Nor had she gained any understanding of them.

Her companion felt Ko's disappointment and made a halfhearted attempt to soothe it. :**You tried your best, Ko. Perhaps Mog was correct. Perhaps they are not intelligent.**:

:**I cannot accept that, Tef. They must be intelligent. They MUST be.**:

There was one observation that Ko kept to herself. This longer exposure to the mysterious visitors had given her the time to notice that there was something

163

different about the tallest one. It was not like the two smaller ones, which seemed to be subservient to it. The colors she felt from the tall one were somehow cooler, less variable. Except for the fact that it seemed to behave in much the same ways as its companions, Ko might have doubted that the tall one was a live thing.

Perhaps this different one is the key, she thought. She would not give up. She *could* not. But she knew her time was running out.

With gulps of total disbelief, Gina and Ken stared at each other, then became aware that the two tiny sparkles that had seemed to precipitate the magical transformation were now hovering above them. The sparkles circled overhead, and Gina twirled in place with them, as if joined in some improvised ballet. Then they spiraled up into the darkness and vanished, leaving her lightheaded. Data steadied her with a hand on her shoulder.

"Commander," Kenny said, his voice once again husky with fear, "if those things—whatever they are—did all this to solid rock—what if they change all these tunnels around? We might *never* find our way back."

"That is a very real possibility, Mr. Kolker. In which case, haste would seem to be in order."

"In other words," Gina said, "let's get the hell out of here."

Chapter Thirteen

JEAN-LUC PICARD held up a long loaf of bread, fresh from the oven, still warm to the touch, perfectly crusted yet soft inside. He broke off a hunk, and gave it to Captain Arit. The splendid and varied aromas of baking filled the tiny *boulangerie*—the sweetness of the pastries, the hearty smell of the bread—and brought a smile to Picard's face.

The baker behind the counter was a tall, barrelchested old fellow with white hair and a bushy moustache that remained incongruously dark. As usual, he had accented his florid complexion with powdery streaks from the flour on his hands. In his childhood, Picard had wondered if everything in Henri's house, including his wife and gaggle of children, were similarly streaked. The old baker reached for a giant mitt and, with a proud flourish, slid another fresh rack of bread loaves out of the big oven at the back of the shop. The heat of the oven produced beads of sweat that trickled down through the powder on his face. "Jean-Luc," he called as he patted away the dampness with his white sleeve, "how is it?"

"Wonderful—*c'est toujours delicieux,* Henri," Picard said with a reminiscent grin. "Can I pay you next time?"

Henri replied with a short burst of staccato laughter that set his belly and jowls aquiver. "Just like when you were a boy, eh, Jean-Luc? *Toujours un petit polisson!*"

"What did he say?" Arit whispered, feeling a bit left out.

"He said I was always a little rascal. When I was a boy, I would stop in here every week and pick up a loaf of bread. I would always ask if I could pay next time, and Henri would always say yes."

"And *did* you pay next time?"

Picard turned sheepish. "I'm ashamed to say I didn't. But Henri and my father were good friends, and I am quite sure Henri got his share of free wine from our vineyards." They reached the door and Picard opened it, tripping the little bell mounted overhead, causing it to jingle a merry farewell.

"Merci, Henri. Au revoir."

The jolly baker waved. *"Au revoir, Jean-Luc.* Come back soon, and say hello to your family for me!"

The two spaceship captains exited onto the cobblestoned main street of the sleepy village, nestled in a gentle valley between rolling hills. Vineyards spread into the distance in every direction.

"What did you say the French word for 'bread' is?" Arit asked.

"Pain," Picard said, pronouncing it "pan," with the inaudible French "n" swallowed at the end. He listened approvingly as she repeated it. "Very good."

"So is the bread," she said, swallowing the last bite.

He handed her half of the rest of the loaf and took a bite from his own chunk. As villagers on foot or riding bicycles went about their business, Picard and Arit strolled past shop windows shaded by awnings, then stopped at a sidewalk café and sat at a table facing the street. A pretty young waitress with raven hair and blue eyes appeared with two stemmed glasses and a bottle of red wine. With a flirtatious smile at Picard, she poured for them, then moved on to other tables and patrons.

Picard appraised the bottle label. "Not a great vintage, but reasonably good." He took a taste and gave it a genteel swish around his mouth before swallowing. "So what do you think of my home village?"

Arit sipped the wine and smiled at him. "A refreshing distraction, Picard—which *is* what you had in mind, isn't it?"

Picard gave a confessional shrug. "Guilty as charged. Once the immediate threat to your ship had been taken care of, I thought a bit of diversion might benefit both of us while we waited for Commander La Forge's evaluation to be completed."

"Well, I hate to admit it, but you were right. Our basic conflict has yet to be resolved. Some time to clear our heads couldn't hurt." She shook her head in amazement as she glanced around. "But I still can't believe we're on your ship's holodeck. I've never seen technology like this. It all seems so real."

"Well, it is real, in a sense. This is a perfect reproduction of what Labarre was like the last time I was home, just a few months ago. Right down to Henri and the lovely waitress."

Arit gazed wistfully off into the distance. "Home," she sighed. "Could this holodeck of yours recreate my hometown?"

"It can simulate any setting, real or imaginary, if the computer has enough information to design a sufficiently complete matrix. Why do you ask?"

"Mmm, no special reason," she shrugged. "You know, my daughter never got to see Tenira. She was born after we resettled. She has no idea where she came from, what her homeworld was like, before . . ."

As her voice trailed off, Picard could sense her regret, but the intercom tone sounded before he could say anything sympathetic. "Riker to Captain Picard."

Picard touched his insignia communicator. "Picard here. What is it, Number One?"

"Geordi is ready with his evaluation and he's on his way to the bridge."

Picard downed the rest of his wine and stood. "In that case, so are we."

"Correlation complete," the computer said in its flat female voice, then displayed a graph on the viewscreen with a green indicator line showing energy output readings recorded by the *Enterprise* sensors during the time the ship had been orbiting Domarus Four.

Geordi La Forge glanced around the conference-lounge table at Riker, Beverly, Worf, Picard and the Teniran captain as they waited for him to share his findings. The chief engineer traced his finger along the graph, beginning at the far left where the green line was virtually flat, hardly registering at all.

"Now, back here, when we first entered orbit, most of this is just normal background radiation." The indicator line rose at a gentle angle. "Then here—

that's where something started happening, a noticeable increase in energy output."

"Caused by what?" Riker asked.

"I have no idea, Commander," Geordi said. As he slid his finger to the right, he reached a sudden peak in the graph, which matched up with a blinking red point. "Then we get to here—the first big jump in energy output coincides exactly with the first appearance of that chromatic energy phenomenon and the disappearance of the shuttlecraft."

The rest of the graph showed a continuing rise in energy output over time, marked by occasional and irregularly spaced peaks separated by long, flat valleys. As time elapsed, Geordi pointed out, the peaks were coming with greater frequency and intensity.

Dr. Crusher's brow furrowed in concentration. "It's almost like contractions at the end of pregnancy."

"Doctor," Picard said wryly, "are you suggesting something is about to give birth down there?"

"I was just commenting on the parallels, Captain."

"Commander La Forge," Arit said, "each energy peak has a corresponding flashing marker. I take it that means that each peak is concurrent with a specific and major incident, like the various unexplained appearances and disappearances of Captain Picard and myself?"

"That's right, Captain." Geordi pointed to one of the middle peaks, higher than the others and of considerably greater duration. "This one occurred at the time of that quake you both experienced, and persisted through much of that overnight period—"

"Meaning," said Riker, "that it matches up with the apparent creation of that new mountain range?"

"Exactly, sir," Geordi said.

Picard rubbed his chin pensively. "Mr. La Forge,

are you theorizing that those bursts of chromatic energy caused these specific events?"

"We can't be conclusive about cause and effect, Captain," Geordi said. "But there's almost no question that they're related in some way."

"Computer," Picard said, "estimate probability of causative relationship."

"Ninety-two point four-six percent probability."

"Hypothesis: that these incidents catalogued by Chief Engineer La Forge represent attempts at communication by as-yet unknown sentient life forms on Domarus Four. Confirm or refute."

Eyebrows rose around the table as Picard's inferential leap caught the rest of the conferees by surprise. The computer took only an instant to consider the query and formulate its reply.

"Insufficient data for conclusive deduction," it said.

"All right. Just calculate the probability, then," Picard said with a casual wave of his hand.

"Eighty-six point two-two-eight-six percent probability that this hypothesis is correct."

"Do you really think there's that kind of pattern here, Jean-Luc?" Beverly asked.

With a contemplative breath, he mulled the question. "Perhaps it's a hunch as much as anything in the way of firm evidence, but I do believe there is an intelligence at work on Domarus."

"An intelligence?" Beverly repeated. "What kind?"

"If it was a life-form like our own," Riker said, "we'd probably have picked up at least some hints of that by now. So, more than likely, it's nothing like us."

Picard nodded. "Agreed. If, for the sake of argument, we accept that foundation, then it is certainly within the realm of possibility that this intelligence—whatever its form—would at some point try to communicate with us." He paused and glanced around the room. "Reactions?"

"If this theoretical intelligence *is* totally different from us," Arit said, "it is quite probable that we and it would not speak anything even remotely resembling the same language."

"Which fits in with your question to the computer," Beverly said to Picard. *"Is* something trying to communicate with us in a way we're just not understanding, or even realizing?"

Picard got up from the table and approached the computer screen. "If we follow this course of reasoning, and allow ourselves to be guided by Geordi's graph, then there is a suggestion that quite a few of the specific 'peak incidents' came about in response to actions taken by the *Enterprise* and the *Glin-Kale*—or at least considered by Captain Arit or myself." He pointed to a succession of the blinking marker spots. "Here, for instance, is our initial confrontation over the shuttlecraft—here, here and here, our escalating verbal hostilities. Each incident, followed immediately by the appearance of the chromatic energy field—and that, in turn, followed by our abrupt transfers to the planet and to each other's vessels."

"Picard," Arit said, leaning forward, "are you saying that this intelligence that we can't understand . . . somehow understands *us* . . . and keeps meddling in our encounters?"

"So it would seem."

Beverly let out a low whistle. "Am I the only one who finds that a bit unnerving?"

Captain Picard glanced her way. "Unnerving? How so, Doctor?"

"Something we can't see—can't locate—can't talk to—and it may be shouting right in our ears? Or at

171

least, it *thinks* it is. And we just don't get it. If it were me in that position, I'd start to get a little frustrated after a while. And frustrated intelligence can turn hostile."

"I agree with Dr. Crusher," said Worf, breaking his silence.

From the flicker in her eyes, Picard had the distinct notion that Beverly was not all that comfortable to find herself in concurrence with the Klingon security chief. On such matters as contact with mysterious life-forms, she tended toward the open-handed approach, while Worf—by virtue of instinct and job training—preferred the well-formed fist. "Would you care to elaborate, Mr. Worf?" said Picard.

"The forces originating on the planet pose a potentially lethal danger to the *Enterprise.* If we *are* dealing with a form of sentient life we do not understand, it will be that much more difficult to defend ourselves if this life form does become hostile."

Captain Arit thumped her hand on the table. "I also agree with that, Picard."

Picard's mouth thinned to a thoughtful line. "Hmm. I acknowledge the value of such caution, but I see no alternative to taking the risk. If we are to solve this riddle, retrieve our shuttle and determine if Domarus is safe for the Tenirans to settle, then we need more information."

Arit looked at him. "And how do we go about getting it?"

"By making a greater effort to stimulate communication. The more response we are exposed to, the more likely we are to figure out a key to understanding who or what we are dealing with."

A dubious expression crossed Arit's face. "What do you mean, 'stimulate communication'?"

"I think I see what you're getting at, sir," Riker said. "If our actions caused who or whatever is on Domarus to respond with those chromatic energy bursts—"

"We should be able to elicit similar responses," Geordi cut in, "by doing more of what we did before—responses we'll be ready for."

"Responses we can then study closely," Picard said, "and perhaps decipher. Any comments or dissents?" There were none and the captain of the *Enterprise* stood. "Then let's formulate a strategy. And remember—the lives of our missing away team and five thousand surviving Tenirans depend on our success."

Chapter Fourteen

"MOTHER, TELL ME what the *Enterprise* is like," little Keela demanded. "Is it nicer than the *Glin-Kale?*"

As she looked at her impatient child, Captain Arit wore an expression fairly common to mothers, a mixture of amusement and exasperation. "Yes, Keela . . . I'm afraid it's much nicer than the *Glin-Kale.*" She tried to get on with the task of reorganizing her desk, sorting through the data pods that seemed to replicate themselves into a veritable population explosion whenever she was too busy to review them on a timely basis.

But she knew what was on them—reports from department heads telling her how this or that system was about to fail, or had already done so. How they were about to run out of spare parts, or had already done so. How they struggled to get along without properly trained crews.

Maybe it was time to dispense with these blasted reports entirely. On a vessel as crippled as the *Glin-*

Kale, it was no longer news when something failed. No, the surprise was when something actually *worked.*

"Is it less crowded than our ship?"

"Hmm?" Arit had gotten totally distracted. "Was it what?"

"Mother." Keela drummed her fingers on the desk, the way she had seen her mother do, and she jutted a lower fang over her upper lip, giving her a snaggle-toothed look of annoyance. "You aren't even listening to me."

"I'm sorry . . . yes, the *Enterprise* is less crowded than this ship. Much less crowded. And I do think you'll have a chance to visit over there."

The little girl's air of jaded impatience vanished, as she clapped her hands in anticipation. "Really? When?"

"Not just yet." As she spoke, Jevlin entered the office cabin and boosted Keela up for a hug, then set her down. "Now run along and play, Keela," said her mother. "I have to discuss some very important things with Jevlin and Valend Egin."

"Egin!" Jevlin sputtered. "Why him?"

"Because he is the only valend, and it's a courtesy . . ." She paused, bent close to Jevlin's ear, and muttered the rest so Keela wouldn't overhear. ". . . no matter what we really think of him. Keela— go—*now.*"

"Yes, mother," the girl sighed, and she retreated to the family quarters next door.

When the door slid shut behind Keela, Jevlin permitted himself to mutter a prefatory curse. Then he said the valend's name as if it were also a curse. *"Egin.* Where the devil is he? He's always late, like he thinks he's royalty or something."

* * *

Egin, the only surviving member of the Teniran government council, stood before the mirror in his cabin dressing alcove. With a tarnished gold comb, he fluffed his silvered hair, adding back some of the fullness that age had removed. Then he opened a worn velvet case, took out an official pendant and hung it around his neck.

"There. How do you think your grandfather looks, Vik?" He turned toward a lanky boy in his mid-teens, dressed in a jacket too tight across the shoulders and knickers too short for his legs. He looked like he was wearing garments belonging to a younger brother, but they were his, long since outgrown. Like everyone else on the *Glin-Kale,* he had to be content with what he had.

The boy flashed a grin with a gap where one lower fang should have been and reached over to even up the pendant's heavy gold chain. "You look like the First Valend, grandfather."

Egin coughed to clear a hoarse rattle from his throat. "Do you think our illustrious captain will treat me with the respect due our leader?"

"If she knows what's good for her, she will."

"Hmmph. Well, she usually doesn't," Egin muttered ironically. Then he swept a hand toward the door. "Walk with me, Vik."

They left the cabin, the boy at his grandfather's elbow as they strolled down a corridor as crowded with huddled refugees as the rest of the ship. People rose to greet their First Valend as he passed by, and Vik beamed with pride.

One old woman grabbed Egin's hand and held it. "Valend Egin, what is happening to us? We thought we'd reached our new home." Other shabby emigrés gathered around him, touching his arms and hands and shoulders as if trying to draw solace from the dim aura of his office.

"Yes," said a younger woman with a hollow-eyed toddler clinging to her neck. "We saw the planet from the windows. Is it ours?"

Other haunted voices echoed in his ears, and Egin listened solemnly. Then he gently withdrew from their grasp and held up his hands in a wordless call for attention.

"I believe we have reached our promised land, the refuge from suffering that we've sought for so many years."

A ragged cheer went up from those closest to him, but he motioned for quiet. "However," Egin continued, "some of our other leaders are paralyzed by fear. They are intimidated by outsiders who have their own agenda. You know, if I had been your First Valend years ago, I never would have struck our fatal bargain with Ziakk. I never would have—"

"Make them let us go home," the young mother said, uninterested in the self-serving trip through the past he was about to begin. She had more immediate concerns. "My baby needs a home."

Egin placed his hand on the young woman's forehead in benediction. "We all do. And we shall have one, soon. Right now, I am on my way to the meeting which may very well decide our fate."

"Then go," said the older woman. "Go with our prayers . . . go with God."

Jevlin lowered himself slowly into Arit's desk chair and rested his walking stick against the wall. "Cap'n, we can't wait all day—what happened with Picard over on that starship of his?"

"You're as impatient as Keela," Arit scolded. "We have to wait for Egin to—"

Just as she said his name, the plump First Valend waddled into the cabin. "You know, Arit, you really should have come to *my* quarters."

"This isn't an audience, Egin," Jevlin said, "it's a damn briefing, so just sit y'rself down."

"All I meant was that my quarters are more spacious, more comfortable and far less utilitarian." He wiped a disapproving finger along the dusty metal frame of the chair before sitting. "And considerably cleaner, as well, I might add."

With Egin finally settled at Arit's desk, across from the first officer, the captain filled them in on the lengthy conferences in which she had taken part aboard the *Enterprise*.

"You told them about our past?" Jevlin protested. *"Why,* Cap'n?"

"Why not, Jevlin? A secret is only worth keeping if it has some value or gives you some advantage. This secret did nothing for us."

"But you revealed our military weakness," said Egin with a reproachful cluck of his tongue.

Both officers flashed quick glares at him, though for different reasons. "That's what I was going to say," Jevlin muttered, not at all happy about discovering that he and Egin had similar disagreements with Captain Arit.

When Arit continued, her clipped tone betrayed a growing displeasure with both men. "Fear of revealing weakness implies that such revelations seriously impair one's battle chances. I'm sure it was already quite apparent to Picard after his visit here that the *Glin-Kale* stood no chance whatsoever against his starship.

And if you two don't realize that, then you are both fools."

Egin waggled a prim finger of objection. "See here, Arit—you can't talk to the First Valend like that."

"That's the beauty of it—I can talk to the First Valend any way I please. Now shut up, Egin."

Jevlin let out a wheezing chuckle.

"You, too, Jev," Arit said, silencing him with a nasty glance. Then she went on with her briefing, explaining in detail the evidence discussed with Picard and his officers, and the conclusions they'd reached about the likelihood that sentient life not only existed on Domarus but had been trying to make contact. By the time she was done, it was quite clear that, for the most part, she agreed.

It was equally clear that Jevlin and Valend Egin did not agree at all, and they burst forth with a discordant clamor of criticism, each trying to outshout the other.

At first, Arit tried her best to respond to the barrage. Then she got angry. Quickly, she reached for Jevlin's walking stick, swung it high and slammed it down on the desktop with a resounding crash that made both men jump. But more important, it stunned them into silence long enough for her to regain control of the situation.

"I'll give you each time for one main objection. Jevlin, you first." When he hesitated, she prodded him with the walking stick. *"Now."*

"How do you know Picard's real goal isn't to make Domarus unfit for us to inhabit?"

"I don't. Your turn, Egin," she said, leaving Jevlin open-mouthed.

Egin stood to make his point. "What proof do you have that you were told the truth about all this on the *Enterprise?*"

"None at all. There—that's done—now let's—"

"Cap'n!" Jevlin roared. "Y're going against every lesson we've learned, and y'haven't answered a single question."

This time, Arit silenced her friend with a piercing look. When she replied, her voice was quiet. "I have one answer, for all objections. My instincts tell me that these people are different . . . that they *can* be trusted. Besides, you both overlook a critical reality. We don't have the power to stop the *Enterprise* from doing whatever Captain Picard chooses."

"All right, Cap'n . . . all right," Jevlin said, scratching the stubble on his chin. "Let's say that's true. What do *we* do then?"

"Nothing, Jev. Nothing at all. We wait to see if the *Enterprise* succeeds in eliciting some comprehensible response from whatever intelligence may live on this planet."

"Hmmm," Jevlin chuckled. "Maybe that's not so bad. If whatever's down there gets riled enough, they'll strike back at the *Enterprise,* maybe do away with 'er . . . and maybe we'll be left to do as we please. I like that . . . yes, I think I do."

"It's down this way," Gina called back over her shoulder. Her voice echoed off the rocks as she trotted ahead of Data and Ken, skipping from side to side as she traversed the rough tunnel floor, yet maintaining her footing with the casual grace of a mountain goat. "I'm sure of it . . . we're almost there."

"Gina," Data said, "do not get too far ahead."

But she was right. The tunnel led around a bend, banked down and took them directly to the cavern containing the shuttlecraft. Gina burst into the cave like a marathon runner breaking the tape and threw herself into the arms of a surprised Wesley Crusher as he and Counselor Troi waited beside the shuttle.

Deanna looked Ken and Gina over. "Other than being a little dusty, you two look none the worse for your unauthorized exploration."

"They appear to be fine," Data said.

"Wait until you hear what we saw," Gina bubbled. But something caught her eye at the far end of the cavern. "Ohmygod—look!"

As she pointed, the others turned to follow her finger. Two of the mysterious sparkles turned lazy circles in the shadows just below the cave ceiling.

"They weren't there a minute ago," Wesley said as he took a few cautious steps closer.

Two more sparkles flared into being, as if invisible hands had just struck a pair of matches. Then still others appeared, singly, in twos and threes, floating or dancing in the air above the away team, in a cavern soon brightened by the shivering silver glow of at least three dozen bits of glittering light.

Then they began to swirl and tumble, and they spun out their multicolored strands of pure light, streamers that spiraled and met and blended, seeming to create intricate designs that lasted only seconds before drifting apart.

"It's gorgeous," Gina whispered. "It's like . . . like living art."

"But it looks so random," Wesley said. "I wish it would find a shape and hold it."

"It may look random, Wesley," Data said, "but it is not. I have been able to identify forty-two distinct designs that repeat with a stable cyclic frequency of two one-hundredths of a second."

Wesley gave the android a double take. "Are you sure?"

"Quite."

"Data, that's incredible."

"And far too rapid for the human brain's capacity for comprehension," Data said. "In addition, it appears that new designs are being added to the totality at a regular rate. Such a complex structure that is both consistent and variable suggests—"

"Suggests intelligence," Troi said softly as she gazed at the colored strands.

They all turned to look at her, and Data nodded. "Yes, that is what I was going to say, Counselor. Are you able to sense anything definitive?"

She edged closer to the astounding light show. A brilliant green tendril suddenly reached out and brushed her shoulder, almost flirting with her. Troi gasped in surprise, but remained in place, watching as it curled back on itself, as if beckoning her to join it.

"I do sense—" Deanna took a deep breath. "Life. Not life as I've ever experienced it before. But I do believe they are life-forms . . . and I believe they are sentient."

Data came up beside her, his pale eyes wide with childlike wonder. "Most intriguing . . ."

Egin entered one of the *Glin-Kale*'s observation areas, illuminated only by a pale shaft of starlight coming through the oval window. Not exactly a large chamber to begin with, it had been converted to storage like most other open spaces on the old ship. Crates and barrels were piled from deck to ceiling, leaving only a small clear area directly in front of the windows.

It wasn't much, but at least here he could peek out at the stars and the vast void around them, and find some momentary relief from the pervasive sensation of being crushed together with all the other refugees. The need for such relief was widespread, and there were too many people aboard and too few observation areas, so Captain Arit had been forced to establish a rule: to ensure reasonable access, no one could remain in any observation nook for more than fifteen minutes.

At some times, there would be long lines of Tenirans waiting for a turn at a window. But Egin found this chamber blessedly empty and he shuffled in—and promptly tripped over a pair of legs protruding from between a couple of supply crates. Egin's hands flew out and caught hold of a barrel before he could fall.

"Oww!" snarled the owner of the legs as he struggled to get up. His silhouette rose before the observation window. It was First Officer Jevlin. "Don't you watch where y'r stepping, Egin?"

"I—I'm sorry," said the flustered official. Then he smelled the *peroheen* wine on Jevlin's breath and frowned in annoyance—*why am I to blame?* "You shouldn't be lying in ambush, you drunken sack!"

Jevlin clenched one fist—the one not holding the bottle—and gave serious consideration to cold-cocking Egin before another word was said. But the purple wine tasted so good after all the time he had been away from it that his hostility was overcome by a rush of comradeship. As he reached out with his free hand, Egin flinched, obviously expecting what Jevlin had initially thought of delivering.

But the fist had relaxed, and Jevlin clamped a nonhostile hand on Egin's shoulder. "There's enough room for two here. Seems to be an off-hour for observin' the stars."

Egin remained wary, unaccustomed to anything resembling a welcome from the old first officer. They stood at the window in uneasy truce, both looking out at the tranquil globe the *Glin-Kale* orbited.

"I thought you'd given up the *peroheen*," Egin said.

"So did I. But special occasions call for special measures, eh?" He held the bottle of purple liquid up, offering to share that as well as the window.

Egin hesitated, then shrugged. "Oh, why not?" He accepted the bottle, and took a swig.

"So," Jevlin said after a silent pause, "what do you think is going to happen?"

"I honestly don't know. What do you think?"

"You're asking me?" Jevlin took the bottle back and helped himself to a thoughtful sip. "I'm just a star sailor. What do I know about momentous decisions? That's your department, eh?"

Egin's expression softened into an ironic smile. "No, not really. I know you and the captain think I'm a pompous fool. And you're right. Sometimes I am. But not so much the fool that I don't know why I'm the First Valend—because I happened to survive."

Jevlin chuckled. "Is that wine, or truth serum?"

"Do you know what I like the most about being First Valend?"

"No . . . what?"

"That it makes my grandson proud of me. If that planet out there does turn out to be our new home— or some other planet does—what I would most like to do is tell stories to the children."

"Stories?" Jevlin said with a quizzical squint.

"Yes. Tell them what Tenira was like. Somebody has to do that, to keep the past alive—the good things, especially. God knows we've seen enough of the bad. There aren't that many of us left who remember the old days, Jevlin."

Jevlin pursed his lips and let out a contemplative

belch. "You mean, like you and me. Hmm. I guess you're right about that. Hmm. Y'know, we're agreeing more'n we used to."

"So we are," Egin said with a nod. "Miracles do happen."

"I suppose."

"Now it's your turn, Jevlin."

"My turn for what?"

Egin held the bottle high. "Truth serum."

"Oh." Jevlin's brow scrunched into a grudging frown. "Fair is fair, I suppose. Well . . . when you mentioned your grandson, I was thinking at least you've got a family. It's been many a year since I sat down with kin. They're all gone now. I don't really have anyone to tell my stories to."

"They don't have to be told to blood kin, Jevlin. Most anyone would listen. I'll wager you've got some interesting tales to tell."

"Mmm . . . I'm not so sure about that."

"We'll have to let our audience judge, once we've got someplace to call home. Thanks for the wine."

"Don't mention it . . . *especially* to Cap'n Arit. I'd hate to disillusion her about my willpower."

Chapter Fifteen

"I DON'T KNOW how you do it, Captain," Riker said as they sat side by side at the heart of the *Enterprise* bridge.

"What is that, Number One?"

"I don't know how you wait so patiently at times like this."

Picard's eyes twinkled with a glint of amusement. "Didn't some elderly schoolmistress ever tell you in your youth that patience is a virtue?"

"I do recall one teacher using those very words, sir," Riker said with a sly smile. "Elizabeth Fallon . . . and she was anything but elderly."

"I take it the seed of her suggestion did not take root?"

"Not exactly. If anything, she made me more impatient."

"How so?"

Riker stretched his long legs. "I was fourteen . . . she was twenty-five . . . and I couldn't wait until I was old enough to go out with women like her."

Picard chuckled, but the quiet moment was cut short by Worf's rumbling voice from the tactical station behind them. "We are ready, sir."

Geordi La Forge stood at the Klingon's shoulder. "It's the planetary equivalent of tapping 'em on the shoulder, Captain. No damage potential to the planet or anything down there."

"Phasers set for wide beam dispersion," Worf said, "random targeting at five-second intervals, power levels at point-five percent—"

"And shields at maximum power," Geordi added.

"Very well, gentlemen," Picard said, leaning back in the command seat. "Initiate firing sequence."

Geordi returned to his engineering alcove and Worf keyed the computer to follow the preprogrammed sequence.

From her bridge aboard the *Glin-Kale,* Captain Arit watched in thoughtful silence as a pair of phaser beams lanced out from the *Enterprise* saucer section, aimed at the planet surface below, specifically the region around the missing shuttle's last campsite. For five seconds at a time, each beam struck a spot on Domarus, then bounced harmlessly to new coordinates.

Jevlin stood alongside the operations console at Arit's left and peered over the shoulder of Mahdolin, the young woman still on watch at that post. Together, they watched sensor reports on what the *Enterprise* was doing.

"I can spit with more power than they're using, Cap'n," the old first officer said disdainfully.

"That's the idea," Arit said, her eyes never wavering from the main viewscreen. "If there is anything down there, Picard doesn't want this to look like an attack."

"More like a *tickle*," Mahdolin muttered.

"Mind your post," Arit said.

"Yes, Captain."

"I agree with the girl," said Jevlin. "I don't know what Picard thinks this is going to accomplish."

Arit leaned forward, elbows propped on her knees. "We'll soon find out."

The gentle volley lasted one minute, then ceased. Picard stood and turned toward Geordi's monitoring station. "Any results, Mr. La Forge?"

The chief engineer shook his head. "Negative, Captain. No response at all. Should we advance to level two?"

"No need for haste," said Picard. "Why don't we see what happens if we repeat phase one."

Worf restarted the computer-controlled cycle of phaser firings, and the captain watched on the viewer as crisp bolts of energy shot from his starship down to the planet. Picard knew the low intensity of these brief phaser bursts would barely ruffle the long hilltop grass bowing before a Domaran breeze. Unfortunately, he could not know whether this theoretical sentient life for which they searched would notice.

"Ahh," Picard murmured, interrupting his own musing. "What do you make of that, Will?"

Riker got to his feet and joined Picard beneath the bridge's central dome as they watched the viewscreen with growing interest. In the midst of this second volley, they saw the sudden formation of what appeared to be a force field just above the Domaran surface. Patches of pulsing energy bloomed at the point of phaser impact, intercepted the phaser beams as they sliced through the planet's atmosphere, then converted them into haphazard knots of energy which simply reflected back out into space before dissipating into an iridescent mist.

"Maybe we *are* getting somebody's attention down there after all," Riker said as the computer completed the programmed firing sequence. "Geordi, analysis?"

La Forge referred to his instrument readouts. "Visually, the effect looks a little different, but the fingerprint of the structural particle pattern is virtually identical to the chromatic energy pulses we've been encountering all along."

"Good . . . very good indeed," Picard said. "Then this response we have just seen may very well be coming from the same source as the chromatic energy phenomenon."

"Well, I'll be darned," Geordi said out loud, though his tone made it clear he was talking to himself as he skimmed some new data printing out on his screen.

Riker looked over to him. "Geordi, what is it?"

"Whatever formed that reflective force shield wound up *absorbing* sixty percent of the energy in those phaser beams."

Picard and Riker both circled up the deck ramp and approached La Forge's engineering console. "Absorbing?" Picard repeated. "Wouldn't it be normal for a large percentage of the phaser energy to be lost in such a process of reflection?"

"Yes, sir, except."

"Except what?" Riker wanted to know.

Creases of amazement crossed Geordi's forehead. "For the first twenty seconds of the shield's reaction, it actually managed to reflect *all* of our phaser energy— one hundred percent—which is more than a little unusual. Then, within *one second,* the percentage of reflected energy dropped right down to forty percent, with no variability after that for as long as our firing continued."

Captain Picard frowned. "Where did the missing sixty percent go?"

"I'd say it went right into whatever was creating the force shield."

"Lieutenant Worf," Riker said, turning to the security chief, "what readings are you getting from that force shield now that we've stopped firing?"

Worf's shoulders hunched as he checked and rechecked the ship's sensors. "No readings at all, Commander . . . as if the shield no longer exists."

"Are there any power readings from any kind of local generator," Riker asked, "or any power source that might be producing this shield?"

"Negative. There are no power readings now of any sort."

"What about before we started firing?" said Riker.

"Nothing, sir—before or after our firing sequence."

"Only during," Riker said. "This is damned strange, Captain. There's no previous sign of this kind of power generation—then this force shield just pops into existence out of nowwhere—*still* without a detectable source of power."

"Strange indeed," Picard agreed with a thoughtful grunt as he considered these latest observations. *Something* down on Domarus had managed to project an effective force shield—and proceeded to absorb the *Enterprise's* phaser energy. Interesting, but by no means conclusive. And the results of this initial experiment had failed to produce any progress toward Picard's main goals—establishing communication with any Domaran life-forms, and rescuing the missing away team and shuttle.

The captain let out a determined breath. "Mr. La Forge, Mr. Worf—advance to level two."

"Aye, sir," Geordi replied. "Five percent phaser power, ten seconds per target coordinate."

"Ready, Captain," Worf said.

Picard nodded as he and Riker returned to their seats. "Fire."

Again, the ship's phaser banks cut loose. This time, the protective shield hugging the planet appeared almost immediately. The results were the same—phaser energy deflected without harm. This time, though, with the increased intensity of the incoming weapon beams, the rebounding energy mist reached considerably farther out into space.

Picard and Riker both noted that response. "If full-power weaponry were fired at this protective barrier," Picard said, "I wonder if the reflection would endanger the attacking vessel?"

"I was just wondering the same thing," Riker said. "That would make this—whatever it is—a pretty effective passive defense system. Let's hope we don't have to find out *how* effective."

"Captain," Geordi said, "this time, it absorbed *seventy* percent of our phaser energy."

"Hmm. Where is all this absorbed energy going?"

"Good question, sir," Geordi agreed.

"See if you can find an answer to it."

"I'm already working on it, Captain."

The light show in the cavern continued unabated, now filling a sizable volume from floor to ceiling. Wesley, Gina and Ken had fanned out with activated tricorders, scanning and recording everything from different angles.

Then the sounds began—feeble and distant at first,

like far-off wind chimes jangled by some faint zephyr, then swelling in amplitude. Data wandered a few steps closer, staring up at the wheel of whirling colors and glittering sparks.

"Counselor," he called back, "are you sensing anything from the chromatic energy mass?"

"Yes, I am. In fact, it's rather overwhelming," she said, wincing a bit, as if trying to fend off a storm of voices shouting in her ear.

A concerned expression clouded the android's face and he came over to her. "Are you all right, Counselor?"

"Yes, Data, I'm fine," she smiled as she gave him a reassuring squeeze on his arm. "It's like . . . well, imagine being at a crowded, noisy party with music and dancing and a thousand people trying to talk all at once."

Data nodded. "Ah. I have been at such gatherings. The decibel level can reach a magnitude potentially damaging to human hearing."

"Fortunately, I have built-in filtering abilities that protect my empathic 'hearing' from that sort of risk. But that doesn't prevent it from being somewhat unsettling."

"Still, we must be careful."

"I will be."

"Can you tell whether we are dealing with a collection of individuals, or a group mind?"

"I can't isolate specific 'voices,'" she said, her lips tightened with frustration. "But I do believe the mass is made up of individuals. I do not think it is a collective mind."

"Have you received any impressions which you would interpret as hostile toward us?"

"No . . . no. There is some fear . . . fear of the

unknown. But the dominant feeling I get is one of . . . intense curiosity . . ." She trailed off, her dark eyes glimmering with the wonder she seemed to be sharing with that alien intelligence. ". . . and delight."

Data's eyebrows arched. "Indeed. Then perhaps it is time for a closer inspection."

"Data!" Troi called. "What are you doing?"

But he didn't answer. Propelled by his own insatiable curiosity, he was already striding directly into the center of the jumble of colors, his face upturned, head swiveling to take in everything going on around him.

Picard paced the deck between Geordi's engineering alcove and Worf's tactical station, his taut tone of voice making his displeasure all too clear. "This is not working as I had hoped."

First Officer Riker sat on the edge of the aft console bank, his arms crossed over his chest. "Captain, I could've sworn I heard somebody say not too long ago that patience is a virtue."

"At times, a highly overrated one, Commander," Picard said with a sharp look. "Do you disagree?"

"About patience? Not at all. About our strategy? A little. I think we're getting some good data we didn't have before."

Picard huffed out a breath, seeming both conciliatory and impatient at the same time. "But where is it getting us? Do we continue on this path, or try something else?"

"Suggestion, sir?" Geordi offered.

Picard responded with an open-handed gesture of invitation. "By all means, Commander."

"Basically, what we're doing is throwing electromagnetic rocks, trying to get a rise out of whatever is down there. If we throw some rocks from different parts of the spectrum, we might get some varied responses."

Riker's eyes narrowed. "You mean photon torpedoes? We wouldn't be able to limit the damage potential as precisely as we can with phasers."

Engineer La Forge shook his head. "I was thinking tractor beam. Pulling instead of pushing."

Captain Picard pursed his lips in reluctant approval. The tractor beam, meant for towing other vessels and small objects, would of course have no noticeable gravitational effect on an entire planet. Still, there would be no harm in trying. "Very well. Make it so, Mr. La Forge."

With phasers at rest, Geordi activated the ship's tractor system, sending the slender beam down to the planet. Since he didn't actually want to pull chunks of Domaran rock and plant life back toward the *Enterprise,* Geordi modulated the beam to essentially cycle it off at half-second intervals—leaving the tractor with enough strength to register as a force of attraction, but not enough to defeat the forces of gravity that anchored things down on Domarus.

It took less than a minute for the planet's enigmatic energy shield to reconfigure itself and repel the tractor beam the same way it had reacted to the earlier phaser fire.

"Mr. Worf," said a determined Picard, "add level-three phaser sequence to the tractor beam—but retarget for different impact sites a thousand kilometers from the point of tractor beam impact. Let's find out how well this shield can stretch."

"Aye, sir."

With a deft touch, Worf's fingers skipped across his keypad, quickly revising the preprogrammed targeting matrix. Then he activated the sequence. The starship's phasers fired at the planet—and almost immediately, the energy shield formed to deflect them.

Geordi's eyebrows rose in appreciation. "That's amazing. Whatever is going on down there, it sure does work well."

Picard turned and marched back toward his seat. "Maintain level-three firing rate."

"For how long?" said Riker, following him down the side-deck ramp.

Picard's expression was determined. "Until something definitive happens."

Chapter Sixteen

As soon as Data waded into their midst, the ribbons of color and the sparkles that produced them parted, forming a buffer around this intruding object so unlike themselves. When he extended his hand toward them, they retreated further to maintain their preferred neutral zone.

Data wanted desperately to establish some form of communication with them. His approach had been based on the assumption that they were not dangerous; and, so far, they had done nothing to alter that view. He hoped that his presence among them would demonstrate that, likewise, he and his companions posed no threat to them or their as-yet unexplained activities.

Then again, all these efforts might simply prove futile. Even if the luminous motes of energy were actually sentient, that was no assurance that they and humanoid species—or androids, for that matter—would ever be able to communicate. There were no guarantees among the laws of nature that wildly dissimilar life-forms could in all instances find common ground on which to build the foundations of understanding necessary for complex exchanges of information.

Some gulfs could not be bridged.

But it was not in Data's nature to be pessimistic. Neither could he be called an optimist, not in the way the word applied to human psychology. As a machine, he had been designed and programmed to be objective, neutral, and unbiased in his appraisal of factual observances of the universe around him.

Still, his innate self-awareness told him that he behaved in a manner that humans would characterize as endlessly hopeful. Perhaps his inability to feel fear or despair just made him appear that way. Or perhaps any being able to objectively approach life, unburdened by self-created demons, could simply not be anything but hopeful.

Though he had given much thought to this puzzle, Data had never reached a conclusion. But he did know this: any given problem had multiple solutions. Permitted the time and opportunity to explore them, he believed he would invariably find one that worked.

One golden sparkle, larger than the rest, hovered slightly off to one side. It caught Data's eye.

The different one, Ko thought. What was it doing? Ko's fellows had drawn back when the different one entered their midst, but no more extreme reaction appeared to be warranted. The different one seemed distinctly nonaggressive. Ko's desire to communicate with these live things swelled; she felt like she was about to burst.

What did the live things think when they saw Ko and

her fellows of the Communion? *What are we to them? Where did they come from, they and their little containers?*

Ko had looked up into the Great Darkness and seen the small points of energy. *They look so much like us—are they other Shapers? Do they too dream and shape their Worlds the way the Shapers of this World do? Do these live things live out there in the Great Darkness with those others Shapers?*

So many questions—I must know the answers . . . even if I die finding them!

A large crimson sparkle swept down from a vantage point near the peak of the cavern ceiling. :Ko! Your time is nearly expired,: said Mog. :Are you ready to admit your failure and submit to the will of the Communion? They must be destroyed.:

Ko spun into a fury. :No! Time is not yet up, Mog—and my efforts are not yet done.:

:What is left for you to do? These things are clearly unintelligent.:

Suddenly, Ko stopped her spin and flared like a small sun going nova. :We will merge.:

With both hands, Data reached out toward the tiny golden star and the frenzy of colors suddenly exploding around it. To his surprise, the swirl of brightness around him did not withdraw. Instead, the colorful maelstrom closed around him.

Then he felt what he could only describe as a tingling sensation racing through his neural circuitry—a rather pleasant sensation, increasing rapidly in intensity.

Suddenly, the bright cocoon encircling him flared to a yellow brilliance and he felt a jolt hit his brain—his eyes bulged, then clamped shut—

198

"Data!" Troi suppressed a scream and reflexively started to rush forward to free him, but Wesley's unexpectedly strong grip held her back. Horrified, they watched as a storm of sparkles coalesced quickly around Data, reeling their colored streamers into a tight translucent shell of shifting hues.

As Data stiffened, the power roiling through the multicolored cloud lifted him, flipped him to a horizontal position, and held him there, shuddering in mid-air two meters off the cavern floor.

Troi tried to control the shiver of terror chilling her. "Wesley! What's happening to him?"

Wesley thumbed his tricorder switches, but the little scanner could only display the gibberish of overloaded electronics. "Dammit! It's not working." He started forward. "I've gotta help him—"

Now it was Troi's turn to do the restraining and she grabbed his arm. "Wesley—*no*—there's nothing you can do."

As they and the others stared helplessly, Data and the web of power and colors entrapping him simply and abruptly winked out of existence.

Still unconscious, still suspended horizontally, Data materialized inside a vault of light, with no apparent walls or boundaries. A pair of the glittering scintillae, the crimson and the gold, attended the twitching android.

Starting at Data's head, the gold one spiraled down the length of his body, then back up, as if examining him. Then it darted in through an ear opening and disappeared. The crimson sparkle, which had been hovering, followed the gold one inside Data's head.

Seconds later, the gold one emerged out the other ear with its crimson counterpart in pursuit.

They pinwheeled away in opposite directions, then

rushed back at each other, colliding in a brilliant flash, flickering in alternating red and gold. Soon, the gold predominated, and then they split apart.

The crimson one flared. :There is no wisdom in this, Ko. You cannot merge with something so unlike us.:

:How do you know? You are too afraid to try. And it is not your decision, Mog. I have told you—this is my Communion—my vision will lead.:

Mog fluttered nervously, seemingly intent on keeping a cautious distance from Data. :There may be dangers.:

:From these things? If they had the power and the will to harm us, they would already have done so.:

:These things are unknown, Ko. You cannot know for certain.:

Ko alighted on Data's forehead, as if daring Mog to draw near. :No, I cannot. But we have the chance to find out. That is what makes this encounter so exciting. To do something we have never done before.:

:That is not our way.:

:Perhaps it should be. According to the Orthody, all choices are mine.:

The crimson sparkle enlarged threateningly, and advanced on Ko. :How dare you quote the Orthody when you violate its spirit! That is your interpretation, Mog.:

:There are no rules for this. This has never happened in any other Communion.:

:And you cannot say what will happen in mine. I warn you—do not stand in my way. Your disapproval means only one thing to me, Mog—that I am right in everything I have done.:

Mog backed off, darkening. :Very well. Merge if you must. When it fails, only you will be destroyed, Ko.:

Like the birth of a Universe, beginning in profound nothingness, Data's mind burst into brilliant life with visions of a world and wonders he'd never seen before. Stripped of all awareness of containment within a body, yet still able to conceptualize himself as Data, his consciousness soared free through a crystal-blue sky.

Falling on a downdraft, invisible wings seemed to thrust him through brilliant white clouds where jagged streaks of lightning surged past him. He followed them down, and the phantom wings leveled him off above a broad plain carpeted with undulating waves of grass. As he skimmed the flat land, the lightning bolts struck the ground and it began to ripple beneath him, rising up to form majestic mountains.

He rose himself, lofted by the winds above the highest peaks, sailing on a trajectory toward a distant, twinkling star. His mind's eye blinked—and when it opened again, the far-off star was now a flaring sun, filling the sky with fire.

He blinked again, and felt himself diving down toward a desolate valley of shifting dunes extending past every horizon. But the sands began to flower and the dunes ran like melted wax, transforming into terraced hillsides lush with tropical growth. Subterranean waters bubbled up to flood the parched valley, and the newborn sea spread wide until it became an ocean.

Then, lifted by the strong wings he could neither see nor control, Data soared again.

Grim-faced, Jean-Luc Picard stood in the center of his bridge, his eyes on the main viewscreen.

"Phaser sequence, level four," said Worf's rumbling voice from behind him, "programmed and ready to initiate."

"Very well, Lieutenant. Fire."

Two seconds after Worf implemented the order, an energized haze, distinctly golden this time, enveloped Picard. A second later, before anyone could move, it and he vanished.

Riker leapt from his seat. *"Cease fire."*

The golden haze materialized inside the Domaran cavern containing the shuttle, and so did Captain Picard, looking more than a little startled once the haze dissipated and he realized where he was, and who and what were there with him in the darkness illuminated only by the away team's lanterns.

Troi and her three companions rushed over to greet him, their expressions a confused mixture of terror and relief, and all of them burst out talking at once. Even Counselor Troi couldn't help joining in, and Picard did his best to sort out the tangle of voices peppering him with questions—

"Captain, how did you find—"

"Captain, where did you—"

"Captain, we thought we'd never—"

"Captain, I can't believe—"

Then he frowned and silenced them with an impatient gesture. "I take it you are all unharmed?"

"Yes, sir, we are," Troi said.

"Where is Mr. Data?" He noticed the quick exchange of concerned glances among the stranded away-team members.

"We don't know, Captain," Troi said. As a prelude, she began to describe the multicolored energy patterns and the unexplained sparkles.

It only took a few moments for Picard to realize the away team and the ships in orbit had shared some parallel experiences over the past couple of days, and he interrupted her. "We saw those same chromatic energy phenomena in space—and I have had several interesting personal encounters myself. Have they done something to Data?"

Troi started again, skipping directly to a condensed account of Data's disappearance, and once again she was interrupted—but this time, by Data's abrupt reappearance, suspended as before inside a blazing halo of golden light.

Picard tried to shade his eyes. "What the devil . . . ?"

His voice trailed off as the yellow blaze quickly faded—and whatever force had been holding Data up also faded, unceremoniously dropping him to the cave floor like a crumpled rag doll. Picard and Troi rushed over to him. Wesley, Gina and Ken started to follow, but the captain waved them away.

"Stay back—we don't know if there's any danger."

Wes activated his tricorder and scanned the side of the cave where Picard and Deanna knelt over the fallen android. "There's no detectable radiation, sir. No other apparent risk factors."

"Thank you, Ensign," Picard said, straightening Data's tangled limbs. His tone made it clear he still wanted them to keep their distance.

Deanna smoothed Data's hair and touched his cheek. Then Picard turned Data's head to one side and peeled back the patch of scalp that concealed some of his diagnostic circuitry. What Picard saw made his blood run cold.

"Dear God," he murmured, swallowing hard. Normally, the tiny lights inside would be blinking in rapid sequence. Now, they were all dark. "He's not functioning . . . we need to get him back to the ship if we're to have any chance of saving him."

He looked up and tapped his communicator. "Picard to *Enterprise.*"

"They don't work down here, Captain," Wesley said. "At least they haven't up till now." He and the others had moved closer despite Picard's caution.

"There must be a way to—"

Deanna gasped. "Captain."

He followed her gaze down to the access opening in Data's head. One by one, the lights began to glow. Then they resumed their sequential flashing. Data's eyelids fluttered open, his head turned, and he sat up to see five faces beaming at him. On his own face, he wore a blissful smile.

"Data," Picard said, letting out a breath he hadn't realized he'd been holding. "Thank God—we thought—"

"We thought you were dead," Troi said.

"To be honest," Data said, "I had entertained that possibility myself."

Ensign Crusher extended a hand and helped the android to his feet. "Thank you, Wesley." Data brushed himself off and resealed the access flap on the side of his head. "Captain, I am surprised to see you here."

"Not half as surprised as I am to *be* here. But that is of less consequence than your condition."

"Though it would probably be advisable to have Geordi run a total diagnostic systems analysis upon my return to the *Enterprise,* I seem to be functioning within acceptable parameters, sir."

"Are you certain of that?"

"Quite certain."

"Data," Troi said, "do you have any idea what happened to you?"

"My sensory and memory circuits seem to have been overloaded by external stimuli, which would account for my brief incidence of unconsciousness. Complete processing and recall will take me a few moments—but I can say that I have just had a most intriguing encounter with the life-forms inhabiting this planet."

Data had barely begun to describe some of his strange visions when a group of at least a hundred sparkles abruptly appeared overhead several meters behind him, accompanied by faint chiming sounds. They glowed in a whole spectrum of colors. An occasional colored tendril floated out of the pack, but compared to earlier displays, the sparkles seemed tentative and passive, as if waiting for something.

Picard pointed over Data's shoulder. "Are those the life forms you mean?"

The android turned. "Yes, sir, they are."

"Data, exactly what happened? Were you able to communicate with them?"

"In answer to your first query, it will take a somewhat lengthy narrative to fully describe what I experienced." He sighed with regret, and his smile faded. "As for whether I was able to establish any meaningful communication, I am afraid the answer is—"

:Yes—he was.: The words seemed to echo through the cavern, spoken in a gender-neutral voice with a faintly musical quality.

Data's eyes widened. "Most interesting."

Wesley stared at the sparkles. "They talk?"

"Not that I am aware of, Wesley," Data said. "Are you saying you heard an actual vocalization?"

Picard gave Data a confused glance. "Yes. Didn't you?"

"No, sir. I received direct input to my sensory analysis node."

"And I sensed it empathically, Captain," Troi said.

"Most interesting indeed, Data." Picard turned and took a few careful steps toward the swarm of glittering particles. "Are you the inhabitants of this world?"

One golden sparkle, larger than the others, emerged from the clump and pinwheeled to within two meters of Picard, where it hovered at his eye level. :Yes. This is our place—our World.:

"What do you call yourselves?"

:In your words, we would be called Shapers. I am called Ko.:

"I am called Jean-Luc Picard. I am Captain of the Starship *Enterprise*. We represent the United Federation of Planets."

:Picard-of-Enterprise. Federation?:

"Why did you capture this ship and its crew?" Picard asked, gesturing toward the shuttlecraft.

:Capture? We did not capture. I felt danger to them—so I brought them here to preserve them.:

Data stepped forward. "Captain, the *Onizuka* was in danger. Had we not been removed from orbit at the time we did in fact disappear, the shuttle might have broken up and the away team might have been lost. So, in a sense, Ko's claim is defensible."

Picard's jaw tightened with mild annoyance. While Data's statement may have been factually accurate, Picard found the timing less than propitious, fearing that it might undercut his questioning of the Shaper about its actions. "That may be true, Ko—but why didn't you release them? Why did you continue to hold them here?"

:I still felt the colors of danger—in you—in your ships. We tried to communicate with you, but you did not understand.:

"The colors of danger?" Picard whispered with dawning comprehension. "Of course . . . the *colors* of danger. The energy patterns we saw as chromatic displays and heard as indefinable sounds—those were your methods of communication?"

:Yes.:

"Then you are correct, Ko. We did not understand. How is it we can understand you now?"

"Captain," Data said, "I believe it was my interaction with the Shapers. Before losing consciousness, I felt an intrusive force enter my central memory core. Evidently, their energy patterns proved to be compatible with my positronic brain impulses."

:I absorbed much information from merging with Data.:

"Why with Data?" Picard asked. "Why didn't you merge with me when you first brought me to your world?"

:You are biological . . . fragile. We feared we would harm you. When I discovered that Data had a different structure, I believed he could withstand the process of merging with less risk to him.:

"Ko," said Data, "there is something I do not understand. Why did you not make your presence known and establish this form of communication when we first arrived on your world?"

:We were still in Interval then.:

"Interval?" Picard echoed.

:What you would call sleep, Captain Picard. Our Interval lasts one thousand of your periodic cycles called years.:

"Wow," Gina said softly. "Where do you—uhh—sleep?"

:Deep inside the World. This Interval had one hundred such years remaining when you awakened us.:

"We awakened you? How did we do that?" asked Wesley.

"Our seismic tests, I suspect," Data said, "our sonic probes of the interior of Domarus. Is that correct, Ko?"

:Yes, Data.:

"Ko," said Data, "humans and other biological life forms sleep mainly to replenish their energy. If I may ask, what is the purpose of your Interval?"

The Shaper hesitated, as if groping for the right way to express herself. :Interval is our time to . . . to reflect on what has been done . . . and . . . to dream of how we wish to shape our world. And when we emerge, that is the work we do.:

"Shaping your world?" said Picard. "What do you mean? We saw no structures of any kind on this planet."

:Structures? What is a structure?:

"Buildings—places to live or work—uhh, canals or waterways for irrigation or transport. Any artificial constructs that are added to the natural landscape."

:I am still uncertain as to your meaning.:

Picard took a deep breath, overriding the frustration he felt at his inability to explain concepts obviously alien to the Shapers. "Beings like ourselves need protection from the elements—from rain and wind and cold temperatures, so we make shelters out of things like wood and rock. We live inside them, much like we are now inside this cavern . . . inside your world. You said you sleep inside your planet during Interval. Where do you stay after you emerge?"

:Everywhere . . . anywhere. We do not need such shelter or protection as you.:

"Hmm. And transportation is something with which you seem to have no problem. So exactly what is it you shape?"

:Ah. I begin to understand. We do not build structures—we shape the World itself.:

"You mean the topographical features," Picard said, "the mountains and the seas and the land?"

:Yes.:

Picard smiled in wonder. "I believe I have witnessed your work—the overnight creation of a mountain range."

"Overnight?" said Wesley. "That's unbelievable. That would take so much energy."

"There is abundant energy available on such a planet as Domarus," Data said, "much as there would be on any planet with an active core and surface features similar to those on Earth. I believe the Shapers are what might be called 'energy-channelers' —able to tap, trap and redirect energy from such sources as geothermal, solar, wind, hydroelectric, the thermal transfer resulting from the contrast between colder seawater at greater depths and warmer currents closer to oceanic surfaces."

"Even the energy from our phasers," Picard added. "In essence, unlimited, eternally renewable power— the sort that would be required to perform such feats as literally moving mountains."

"Energy-channelers would be able to draw upon all such sources," Data said, "and transform it to their own uses."

"Ko, is Data's explanation correct? Is that your nature?"

:It is, Captain.:

Picard rubbed his chin thoughtfully. "A question comes to mind . . . why reshape your world after each Interval?"

:Why?: Ko's tone implied self-evidence. :**Because it is not yet perfect.**:

The reply prompted a sympathetic smile from Picard. "By what standard?"

:**Each Communion—what you would call a generation—has its own standard.**:

"Then the standards must always be changing."

:**That is true, Captain,**: Ko said with a sad flutter in her voice.

"What if perfection is unattainable?" Picard asked.

Ko's answer began with what could not have been anything other than a knowing chuckle. :**Does that mean we should not still try to achieve it? In your own history, have succeeding generations of your people reached goals that previous generations believed unattainable?**:

"Yes. In fact, that has been the nature of humanity —and of most intelligent life-forms we have encountered in our travels."

:**Then we should also try.**:

Picard nodded. "By all means."

The golden sparkle closed most of the remaining distance between itself and Picard. Spinning before him, no more than an arm's length away, it was the size of his hand, made up of radiant spokes of pure energy.

:**In the past, our dreams have or have not become reality based solely on our Shaping. But this Emergence is different, Captain.**:

"How so?"

:The one who leads the next Communion emerges first. The dreams of this leader guide what we do. I lead this Communion. And I dreamed a dream none have had before—and for the first time in the existence of our World, we need outsiders to achieve what I have dreamed.: Ko paused, then continued with amazement growing in its voice. :I do not think you understand the magic of this, Captain. Until these encounters with your people, we did not know that other worlds and life even existed. We thought we were alone in the Universe. We thought our World WAS the Universe.:

Picard glanced up toward the sky he could not see from this cavern, the sky he knew to be out there, above this world as above all worlds, where the sea of stars spread wide, where the warmth of uncountable suns nourished so much life. "You are not alone, Ko, I can assure you."

:Though I do not yet comprehend the nature of this Universe, or understand all that I have learned from Data, I now know the truth of what you say—but we did not know before. And yet, even without that knowledge, I somehow dreamed of things I did not, could not know. And your people came here—and we have met—and that is the magic. So I ask what no Shaper has even conceived of asking before—will you help us shape our dreams?:

Chapter Seventeen

STANDING AT THE science station at the back of the *Enterprise* bridge, Geologist Casby shook her head in complete disbelief as she stared at her small viewscreen. Riker and Geordi stood next to her. Together, they watched a neon-tinted computer graphic of mountains *migrating* across the Domaran landscape.

"Casby," said Riker, "are you sure about this?"

"It's the most unbelievable thing I've ever witnessed . . . but it's real, and it's happening down on that planet *right now.*"

Riker turned to the chief engineer. "Geordi, are you sure our sensors are functioning properly?"

"Absolutely, sir."

"But . . . those mountains are *moving.*" Riker jabbed a finger at the computer screen. "Mountains do *not* move, Casby."

She spread her hands helplessly. "Apparently, Commander, they do here."

Not only were they moving, they were changing

configuration. As the mountain range drifted eastward, several distinct peaks combined into two, then two into one giant mountain looming over a vast expanse of prairie. After that, the impossible motion stopped.

"Casby," Riker asked tentatively, "is that it? Are they finished?"

"I have no idea, sir."

The group at the science console turned when they heard Worf mutter a brusque growl just behind them. He scowled at his own sensor panel. "Commander Riker, an energy anomaly has just been detected off the starboard stern."

"Anything on visual?"

"Affirmative, sir."

"Main viewer, Worf," Riker ordered.

In the seconds it took for Worf to redirect the signal from the starboard scanners, the anomaly had resolved into an intense variation of the by-now familiar chromatic energy apparition. But the colored streamers coiled in on themselves and dissipated— leaving the totally unexpected sight of the shuttlecraft *Onizuka* floating free in space a kilometer away from the starship's tail.

Geordi let out a whoop of joy. "All *right!* Would you look what the cat dragged in!"

"Incoming message, Commander," Worf said. "From what the cat dragged in."

Riker circled down the side ramp to take up a position in front of the command seats. "On audio, Worf."

Among the bridge crew, collective breath remained held—until a welcome voice came over the speaker. "Picard to *Enterprise*. The *Onizuka* is ready to come aboard."

"Riker here, sir. Glad to hear that. Is everyone okay?"

"All fine, Number One. And we've got quite a tale to tell. However, we are going to need a little assistance—the shuttle's engines are inoperative."

"Stand by, Captain. Geordi, a tractor beam, if you don't mi—"

Before Riker could finish his sentence, the glowing tractor beam had already locked on, giving the shuttle its ride home to the hangar deck.

Captain Arit's skepticism showed in her narrowed eyes as she and Picard faced each other on the *Glin-Kale* bridge. "They do *what,* Picard?"

Picard stood before Arit seated in the command chair, with Jevlin and First Valend Egin flanking her. "I found it somewhat difficult to believe myself. But Ko's little demonstration erased all doubts. Seeing mountains actually move before your very eyes is quite a breathtaking experience."

"And this—this—*world-shaping,* this is what they *do?* That's their reason for being?"

"So it would appear. The irony is, while they have the power to physically alter a whole planet—and they have been doing so for as long as they can remember—they cannot leave their world. It's as if they are part of the natural order of things. They could no more be removed from Domarus than the wind could be removed from my world."

"And you say this is their first encounter with life from somewhere else?"

"That's correct," Picard said.

"Let me get this," Jevlin said. "They sleep for a *thousand years* at a time?"

Picard nodded. "Our shuttle crew accidentally

woke a few of them—including Ko, their Communion leader—ahead of schedule. At first, our presence simply piqued their curiosity. Then, when they sensed the shuttle was in danger during our initial dispute, they rescued it."

"But why did they hold it, Picard?" Arit asked. "Why didn't they just transport it back to the *Enterprise?*"

"That curiosity factor. Though they couldn't understand our words, they were able to recognize our conflict, and they guessed that the shuttle was important in some way—and they believed that the *Enterprise* would stay to recover it."

"They were right about that," Arit said.

"But their reason for keeping us in the vicinity was not a hostile one. It was the only way they could think of to gain the time needed to figure out a way to communicate with us."

"So, tell me, Picard," Arit said, "what is this dream of theirs? I can't believe creatures with the power to sculpt a planet instantly would need anyone else to make their dreams come true."

"That's what I thought. But they do. And it is a very simple desire, actually. Now that they know life exists elsewhere, they want to share what they do with beings other than themselves." Unsure of how Arit and the Tenirans would react to what he was about to say, Picard paused for a deep breath. He knew there was only one way to find out. "You need a world on which to live," he said, "and they have one to share. They have invited the Teniran survivors to stay on Domarus."

Picard glanced at the Tenirans arrayed around him, from face to face—and, with some dismay, he found less than wholehearted acceptance. Only Arit looked as if she was ready to call this planet home. She turned to her first officer, whom Picard had by now realized was also her most trusted friend.

"Well, Jev, what do you think?"

"I don't know, Cap'n. We wanted a world of our own. These Shaper things—what if they change their minds about sharing later on? What defense have we got against life-forms that can do what they can do?"

"Hmm. A point worth considering," Arit said.

Egin waddled around to confront her. "I suppose you think you can make this decision without me."

"No, Egin, I don't—as much as I might like to. You and the Guiding Council should certainly discuss this."

The pudgy official blinked in surprise. Her figurative bow in his direction was obviously the last thing he had expected and she had caught him totally off guard. From what Picard knew of Arit's prickly relations with Egin, he had little doubt that was her exact intention.

"After all," she continued, "it's our whole future we're about to decide. Even if I could, I would not want to make that kind of decision alone, Egin. Oh, no. I do not want that responsibility. No . . . I'm more than happy to share it with the Council . . . and especially with you."

"Arit," Picard said, "what is your debate procedure?"

"Well, we'll convene. You can address the Council, Captain, tell them what you've told us. They may have some questions. Then I'll make my statement. And then, since I'm not technically an elected representative, I'll leave them to make their decision."

* * *

216

Arit knew it wasn't much of a council that met in a briefing room doubling as a storage facility. Crates of provisions lined the walls, piled from deck to ceiling, leaving barely enough room for the eight council members to sit around a battered darkwood table on a wobbly pedestal.

On the way down, she had explained to Picard that the House of Valends was the executive branch of Teniran government, while the Guiding Council members were the legislators responsible for carving out the laws that the Valends were supposed to apply to the operation of Teniran society.

As she looked around at the conferees, she was all too aware that this gathering was starkly symbolic of the decimation her people had suffered. Egin was the last survivor of twenty-five Valends, and the eight Councilors here were all that remained of the one hundred who had made the laws back home on Tenira.

The faces around the table were sober ones. The Councilors knew why they had been called together. Arit had not expected overt joy, but she'd hoped for a touch of good cheer, perhaps—or relief, at the very least. After all, the Council was actually going to consider something many Tenirans believed they would never live to see—the decision of whether or not to disembark from the *Glin-Kale* and get on with the building of a new society.

She introduced Picard and endorsed both his honesty and his interest in helping the Tenirans. As he made his succinct presentation of the facts, she watched the faces watching him, searching for some reaction to the facts about Domarus and the Shapers, some hint as to how the Council members might vote.

But there were no such clues to be found. With a sinking sadness, Arit wondered if her people had been emptied of all emotions but fear. Had they lost all capacity for hope? Or were they simply too afraid to risk crushing disappointment again? How strange that people apparently so afraid to dream were being invited to share a planet with creatures whose existence seemed literally to be driven by dreams.

Picard finished his presentation. "I am aware that this is quite a bit to digest in one swallow," he said. "If the members of the Council have any questions, I shall be happy to respond to them."

He was answered by subdued silence. Not a single comment. Arit restrained her urge to jump up onto the table and scream. *How can they just sit there after what he's said? Or are they so numbed by what we've been through that sitting in silence is all they can do?*

And was she really any different herself? *Here you are, sitting all prim and proper and gutless, too—just like they are.*

According to parliamentary procedure, as First (and only) Valend, Egin was nominally the chairman of the session. With an exaggerated gravity that almost made Arit laugh, he looked at his fellow Council members.

"No questions at all? Very well, then. Thank you, Captain Picard. Captain Arit, it is now your turn to make a statement before the Council retires to exercise its sacred right and responsibility of debate and decision. Unless, of course, in the interests of time, you choose to forgo such a statement."

Arit rose with a sarcastic half-smile. "Sorry to disappoint you, Egin, but I will make my statement." She bowed her head, took a deep breath, and let it out slowly. She knew she could address them in only one way—straight from the heart. "I . . . I wish you had been able to show some happiness as Captain Picard briefed you. Because I think this is the most promising day we Tenirans have seen in longer than I would care to remember. We've pressed on, and on, and on— long after we'd lost the will, I think—long after most of us stopped believing we would ever really find a new place to live. So what kept us going? I can't even begin to count the number of times I've asked myself that question. And the answer? Sometimes I think it was nothing more than momentum and habit."

Arit circled the table slowly, at times looking off into the distance, at times gazing directly into the unrevealing eyes of one or another of the Councilors. "Had we not found this planet—had the strange and wonderful events of the past few days not happened—I believe we might have continued as we were, expecting failure and *accepting* it until we were all dead. Maybe even beyond that, if no one had bothered to anchor the *Glin-Kale* to keep her from drifting on into eternity.

"But we are *here* now. And we have a choice to make—to continue the road we know, terrible as it may be, or to stop here and take on a new and per- haps more frightening challenge." Arit paused to absentmindedly nibble on her lip. "You may not believe this, but right up until I opened my mouth to talk to you, I wasn't sure how I felt about this choice. In many ways, it would be easier to leave this un- known world, with its Shaper creatures who are so different from us. What if we can't get along with them? What then? I don't know. Nobody knows.

"But I do know this. It has taken all our courage to

get this far . . . and it will take all the courage we have left to choose to stay." She paused. "But I hope with all my heart and soul that *that* will be our choice."

As anxiously as she had searched the faces of the Council before for some sign of their feelings, she no longer felt that need to know. She had made her own peace with circumstances, and now the rest was up to them.

"Captain Picard," she said, heading for the door, "let's leave the Council to its deliberations."

"What do you think their choice will be?" Picard asked as he and Arit walked slowly down a *Glin-Kale* corridor.

"I honestly have no idea. I'll let you know as soon as they've reached a decision."

"Do you think they'll take long?"

Arit shrugged. "I have no idea about that either." Then she shook her head and laughed briefly.

"You find something amusing?"

"More odd than amusing, I suppose. Tell me something, Picard—as a commander, does it bother you to be out of control?"

His head inclined noncommittally. "To some extent, I suppose. Why do you ask?"

"Just comparing notes. I used to *hate* being even the slightest bit out of control—of anything: my ship, my daughter, my life. But so many things have been so far out of my control for so long now, that waiting for *this*"—she thumbed a gesture over her shoulder, back toward the briefing room where they'd left the Council—"doesn't bother me at all."

"I can understand that."

"I suppose you'll be transporting back to your ship now?"

"Actually, while we waited, I thought we could make some positive use of the time."

"Doing what?"

"Well, I made a conditional promise to your daughter that I should like to keep—if her mother doesn't mind."

"Her mother doesn't mind at all."

"Where would she be now?"

Arit had to think for a moment. "Uhh—she should be in our cabin doing her lessons. I always thought if we ever did find a homeworld, it would help if Keela were properly educated," she said wryly. "Making tea is a valuable skill, but there is more to life than that."

"Sometimes," said Picard. "Sometimes not. Never underestimate the power of a good cup of tea."

They did find Keela in the family quarters. But their arrival caught her by surprise—though she was seated at the computer terminal, it wasn't a formal lesson occupying her. Instead, she had a stylus gripped in her hand and she was using it to draw a picture of the starship *Enterprise*.

"I'm—I'm sorry, mother," she stammered. "I know I should be doing my mathematics studies."

"Normally, I would be quite angry with you," Arit said sternly, "but we actually came to ask you if you'd like to go with Captain Picard to visit his ship."

As much as the Guiding Council's opaque self-restraint had initially bothered Arit, Keela's squeal of pure delight more than made up for it.

Chapter Eighteen

THE DOORS TO Ten-Forward slid aside and Picard led Captain Arit and Keela into the starship's spacious lounge. Two steps inside, Arit stopped and stared, and Picard tried to measure how much of her reaction was appreciation and how much envy.

"When you said 'lounge,' I never pictured anything like this," she said. "A few tables, a little food—but *this* is incredible."

"Mother," Keela chided with a roll of her eyes, "you've used that word over and over since Captain Picard started showing us around the *Enterprise.*"

"For a very little girl," Arit said, casting a reproachful eye down at her daughter, "you have a very tart tongue. I'd suggest you keep it under control, and show a little more respect. Don't *you* find this ship amazing?"

"Of course I do. But one of us has to maintain the family dignity."

Picard stifled a snicker and decided this was the

right moment for a diversion. "Why don't we sit over there by the observation windows?" He guided them to an empty booth and signaled to Guinan at the bar. "Keela, how would you like a very special treat?"

Her brow furrowed guardedly as she gave it some thought—not quite the eager response Picard had been conditioned to expect from his previous shipboard encounters with young children. But then, he reminded himself, Keela was far from typical.

"Is it something childish, Captain?"

"No, not at all. It's true that humans first learn to love it as children, but most of us continue to enjoy eating it—usually in very generous quantities—for the rest of our lives."

"Well, Keela," Arit said, "does that make it sufficiently adult for you?"

"Yes, mother—I think so."

Guinan reached the table and greeted Picard and his guests with her usual smile. "Captain Arit, Keela —welcome to Ten-Forward."

"How do you know who we are?" Keela asked.

Her mother, too, seemed surprised to be addressed by name. Picard knew this was simply one of Guinan's many unexplained knacks—one he had always found amusing. "This is Guinan, the host of Ten-Forward. She knows quite a lot of things she shouldn't know . . . and I have never been able to explain it."

"For instance," Guinan said, "I believe the captain was going to suggest that you both try chocolate ice cream sundaes."

"Correct as usual," Picard said. "And I would like to indulge in one myself."

"Coming right up, Captain."

Guinan left and Keela clambered up onto her

knees, pressing her face to the window for a better view of the planet below.

"Mother, is that going to be our new home?"

"That's what the Council is deciding."

"Would you like it to be?" Picard asked.

Keela drew her lips into a thoughtful line, with one fang left peeking out. "I don't know, Captain. Though after seeing your ship, I'm not sure I want to go back to ours. It's kind of old and dirty—and much too crowded."

Guinan returned to the table with a tray and served three substantial classic sundaes, topped with whipped cream and cherries. Keela grabbed her spoon, but glanced at her mother for final permission. Arit gave her a nod. Still, the girl hesitated.

Picard noticed, then took the lead. "I should warn you, Keela—if you don't eat ice cream quickly, it melts. So I'd suggest we begin." He did, shoveling a large helping into his mouth.

Keela sliced into the double-scoop mound, but came up with a demure sliver of ice cream barely covering the tip of the spoon.

"Captain," Arit said, "Keela isn't terribly enthusiastic about trying new things."

The downy hair of Keela's mane bristled, a reaction Picard guessed to be the Teniran equivalent of blushing.

"Mother, that's *not* true!" Keela dug down again, lifting a heaping spoonful—and then biting off a cautiously tiny mouthful. However, her expression left little doubt that she liked what she tasted, and she happily licked the rest of the spoon. "This is very, very good, Captain."

"I'm glad you like it."

* * *

Wesley and Ken entered Ten-Forward, spotted Picard's group just finishing their round of ice cream sundaes, and crossed directly over to them. "Captain Picard," Wesley said, "we've completed that special special programming assignment you asked us to do."

"Ahh, very good, gentlemen," he said, exchanging a fleeting but significant glance with Arit.

"Did you have enough basic information?" Arit asked.

"Yes, Captain Arit, we did," Ken said. "We think it turned out well—but that'll obviously be up to you."

"Well," she said, "I'm sure you did an excellent job, under the circumstances. Captain Picard assures me that he has complete confidence in your skills."

"Indeed I do," Picard said. "Thank you both for attending to it so quickly."

"You're welcome, sir," Wesley said.

Ken nodded. "Anytime, Captain."

"That will be all for now, gentlemen." He paused. "Unless you'd care to join us in sampling your handiwork."

Now it was the two young men who exchanged a meaningful glance. "Thank you, sir," Ken said seriously, "but we've got some pressing business we need to discuss."

Ken's comment seemed to make Wesley shift uncomfortably. "Maybe we'll join you there in a little while, sir."

"Very well, then. Carry on," Picard said as he and his Teniran guests stood. He gestured toward the exit. "On to the last stop on our tour."

Ken and Wesley remained standing until Picard, Arit and little Keela had gone, then slid into the vacated booth, hunching conspiratorially over the table. Before they'd said anything, Guinan had arrived.

"What can I get you gentlemen?"

"Coffee," Wesley said without hesitation. "Cream and sugar."

"And you, Ken?"

"Uhh . . . coffee for me, too . . . Uhh, make it black."

Wesley stared at him, while Guinan's eyebrows rose in mild surprise. "Two coffees it is," she said. "We've got some delicious pastries . . . I think you might like them."

"Thanks, Guinan," Ken said as she started to turn away.

"On second thought, Guinan," Wesley said, "make mine tea."

"Earl Grey?" she said with a knowing smile.

"Yeah," Wes grinned. Then he refocused his stare at Ken.

"What're *you* looking at, Crusher?"

"Since when do you drink black coffee?"

"I've *always* liked it," he lied. Then he took a deliberate breath. "So . . . what're we going to do about this?"

Wesley shrugged. "How am I supposed to know? This was your idea. I didn't even want to *have* this discussion."

"I just thought it would be more civilized, that's all. I mean, you may be a pain in the butt sometimes, but we are friends. Right?"

"Sure. I guess."

"So," Ken said again, "do you like Gina?"

Wesley's cheeks shaded to a faint red. "Sure I like her. What's not to like? And what about you? Do you like her?"

"I guess so. And . . . now I think maybe she likes me, too."

Wesley looked mildly surprised, both at *what* Ken had said—and the simple fact that he'd actually *said* it. "You think she does? Ken, there's only one way to find out."

"How?" Ken's tone was guarded.

"You *know* how—ask her out."

"But you've already gone out with her."

"We haven't gone *out* out," Wesley said with a dismissive wave. "Not like real dates. We just sort of do things together. It's like I tried to tell you—Gina and I are just friends." As Ken's expression revealed his serious consideration of dawning possibilities, Wes added, "So far."

They were interrupted by Guinan's return with their food and drinks, and they straightened abruptly and tried to make the awkward pause in their conversation seem nonchalant. Wesley could tell that his little addendum had shaken Ken's barely stirring confidence—which was the exact reaction he'd hoped for. In fact, Wesley *had* at times thought of Gina as potentially more than *just* a friend. Perhaps much more.

But he also knew the reality of circumstance, and in all likelihood, he'd soon be leaving the *Enterprise* for Starfleet Academy. As much as he might like Gina, he didn't know if it would be a good idea to start a relationship that would have to be suspended by separation. From everything he'd heard, the first year at the academy was anything but easy. He had been warned to keep distractions to a minimum—and what could be more distracting than a long-distance relationship? I don't need to be pining away for someone when I should be studying my brains out.

Besides, Wesley had no real idea if Gina was interested in a more serious relationship. He'd never asked her. So, all things considered, he'd made up his mind to encourage Kenny to go for it. But he didn't want to make things *too* easy. He hoped the specter of competition might motivate Ken to boldly go where he hadn't had the nerve to go before.

As soon as Guinan had put their tray down and departed, Kenny hunched forward with a worried furrow across his brow. "What do you mean, 'so far'?"

"Oh, nothing. Just that maybe I might ask her out—unless you beat me to it."

"Oh, I don't know. Maybe she doesn't like me," Ken moaned, his resolve deserting him. Then he sipped his coffee, swallowed painfully, and made a disgusted face. "You're right. I don't drink black coffee."

"That doesn't mean you can't ask Gina out. What's the worst that could happen?"

"What's the worst that could happen?" Ken rolled his eyes. "She could say no."

"So? Then you'll be no worse off than you are now."

"Except for my fragile ego getting stomped flat on the deck."

Wesley gave his friend a sardonic half-grin. "Trust me—egos are reinflatable. I read it in one of my mom's medical texts."

Ken managed a laugh, then spotted something across the room that brought a plainly pained expression to his face. "Uhhh—this whole discussion may just have been rendered academic," he said, looking past Wesley.

"Huh?"

"Over there," Ken said, nodding with his chin.

Wes turned to look over his shoulder at a table where a half-dozen young people were seated. And there was Gina, just getting up—her hand clasped by a solidly built young man with wavy hair.

"She's holding hands with *Coggins?* I don't believe this," Wesley said, his disappointment obvious.

"He's got shoulders out to here," Ken whined as he slouched down in his seat. "Do you think she saw us?"

"I don't think so. And they're leaving . . . together." Wesley's eyes tracked Gina and Coggins until they'd reached the door. Then he turned away and leaned forlornly on one elbow. That was when he saw that Ken had perked up noticeably. "What're you staring at?"

Ken not only did not reply—he seemed not to have noticed the question. So Wesley turned again to follow his friend's gaze—and realized that the object of Ken's attention was the only girl still at the other table, with three remaining male companions. She had an ivory complexion, dark hair past her shoulders, and a musical laugh that carried across the room.

"Polly Park," Wes said in admiring appraisal, "has the longest legs I have ever seen."

Ken's mouth quirked in annoyance. "I suppose you've asked her out, too?"

"Nooo. But I've thought about it."

"So we're back where we started from—just with a different girl."

"Why? Were *you* planning to ask her out?"

"Maybe."

Wesley flashed a challenging smile. "She's too tall for you, Ken."

"Oh, yeah?" Ken slid out of the booth and stood, stretching to his full height. "Let her tell me that."

"Where're you going?"

"To ask out Polly Park."

As Ken marched across Ten-Forward, Wesley watched him go. *That's more like it, Kenny,* he thought. *Make it so.*

Picard, Arit and Keela stood on a cliff, overlooking a canyon so deep that they could barely hear the white-water river rushing along the bottom of the gorge. Rainbow mists clung to the canyon walls, and a choir of animals, hidden among peaks and ridges that extended to every horizon, bayed at the setting sun. As a gentle breeze riffled through the manes of mother and daughter, Picard marveled at the bond between them. Even envied it a little.

The Tenirans had struggled mightily to hold together what remained of their families and their society, and he hoped that struggle would soon reach a happy conclusion.

He also found himself thinking about his own family ties. He'd spent all those years—all his adult life, really, after the deaths of his parents—estranged from his brother. How peculiar then that his recovery from the Borg ordeal had not felt complete until his return home to Earth to make his cranky peace with Robert.

That trip had also enabled him to forge new links with Robert's wife Marie, whom he hadn't even met in person before, and with the next generation of Picards, his nephew René.

René, who wants to grow up to be a starship captain like the uncle he barely knows . . . It seemed wondrous to Picard that he could have been such a presence in his brother's family despite his physical absence.

For years, he had considered that separation from his blood relatives an unbridgeable rift. He and Robert were just too different, and too damned stiffnecked to acknowledge the love and respect that bound them together. It had been much easier to perpetuate their differences than to accept them and get on with the business of being brothers.

Picard had made his choices, and he'd been living with them for twenty years or more. Counselor Troi would probably have characterized it as compensation or somesuch, but he had come to believe that his family was right here aboard the *Enterprise*—the officers who were like brothers and sisters and children to him, the people who gave his life shape and meaning.

After that visit home, though, he had happily found that his view had changed. His crew members were still his everyday family; but his new and renewed bonds with his real family back on Earth were what made him more whole than he'd been in years.

And now, the Tenirans were on the verge of being whole once again.

"Tenira must have been a beautiful place," Picard said in a soft voice.

"It was, Picard. It definitely was. I don't know how to thank you for letting me visit it one more time." Arit sighed and glanced down at the child clinging to her hand, looking across the canyon with wide, wondering eyes. "For letting *us* visit it."

"My pleasure."

"Keela, this cliff is where your father and I were married."

"Really?"

"Mm-hmm. We traded our vows at sunset on a day just like this. At least, I remember it like this." With a final lingering look, Arit turned away from her past and started back down a trail that wound through a tall stand of golden trees.

"You can stay a little longer if you like," Picard said.

But Arit shook her head. "No . . . it's time to go."

It didn't take them long to reach the holodeck's access archway. "Save program," Picard said as the door slid aside and they exited into an *Enterprise* corridor.

"Save it?" Arit asked. "Why?"

"Someone may want to visit Tenira again someday."

Picard led them back toward the bridge via a corridor lined with observation portals. As they neared a turbolift, the intercom pager beeped. "Riker to Captain Picard."

Picard touched his uniform communicator. "What is it, Number One?"

"Message from the *Glin-Kale,* for Captain Arit."

Picard looked at her. "Would you like to take it privately?"

"No." She took a deep breath of foreboding. "Whatever it is, you may as well hear it, too."

"Will, transfer it down here, please."

"Aye, sir."

At Picard's nod, Arit found her voice. "Captain Arit here."

"This is Valend Egin, Captain." Egin spoke in an officially momentous cadence. "The Council has finished its deliberations."

"And what have you decided?"

Arit held her breath—and so did Picard.

"The surviving elected government of Tenira has decided . . . to accept the offer of the Shapers."

Arit exhaled and grasped Picard's hand. "Good, Egin. Have you announced it to the ship yet?"

"No, we have not," Egin said. "As Captain, yours is the voice our people are most accustomed to hearing. We felt that should be your duty—and privilege."

"Maybe he's not as bad as I thought," Arit whispered to Picard. "Uhh, thank you, Egin. I'll be returning shortly. We've got a lot of preparations to make. Arit out."

She had let go of Keela's hand during her conversation with Egin, and found that her daughter had drifted over to a nearby observation window. Arit touched the little girl's head. "Back there on Captain Picard's holodeck—that was our old home. And that . . ." She and Keela both gazed out at the blue-white globe just outside. "That will be our new one."

Epilogue

CAPTAIN'S PERSONAL LOG, Stardate 44295.7. An interesting denouement to our surprising encounter at Domarus Four, which shall henceforth be referred to as Mirrillon, the name given to it by its native inhabitants, the Shapers. Our shuttle and its crew have, of course, been returned to us. We have made friendly contact with an unusual life-form previously unknown to us. And the Tenirans have a world to share, a splendid new place to call home.

COMMANDER RIKER strode into a cargo bay buzzing with activity, and found Engineer La Forge surveying a dozen jumbo containers queued up near the cargo transporter. Each one measured four meters high by five on each side, and a half-dozen technicians were busy checking logs listing the containers' contents and making sure they were ready to be sealed.

"Progress report, Geordi?"

"Last shipment, Commander, and it's almost ready to go."

"Good work."

"Thank you, sir," La Forge said casually.

"No, I mean it, Geordi," Riker said, shaking his head in amazement. "I never realized how fast we could mobilize—you and your staff have shipped an incredible amount of survival gear down to Domarus."

"You mean *Mirrillon.*"

"Right. Mirrillon." Riker grinned. "We never had that much of a chance to get used to calling it Domarus, so it shouldn't be too hard to adjust to a new name."

"Especially now that both the Tenirans and the Shapers want Mirrillon to join the Federation. How long before supply ships get here to provide the Tenirans all the stuff we couldn't give them?"

"Two weeks or less. You've scrounged up more than enough to tide them over."

"Well, in spite of the way we met them, they do deserve a break in the luck department."

Riker nodded. "Amen to that."

Picard stood in the center of the *Enterprise* bridge, facing Arit's image on the main viewscreen. "I know the accommodations will not be luxurious, but they will keep you warm and dry."

"Luxury can come in due time, Picard. For now, you have no idea what it means to us just to be able to call someplace, other than the *Glin-Kale,* home. So, for now, warm and dry will be more than enough reason for thanksgiving."

"Thanksgiving," Data said, looking up brightly from his console. "That brings to mind an episode from the history of the United States of America on Earth. Settlers fleeing religious persecution by the nineteenth-century monarchy of England established a colony on the North American continent, known as Massachusetts, and they received considerable assistance from the native population during their early months of residence in what was, to the colonists, a harsh and unknown environment."

The turbolift whooshed open and Riker came onto the bridge in the middle of Data's recitation.

"Following their first year of survival," Data continued, "colony leaders declared a feast of thanksgiving and invited members of the native tribe which had helped them. That feast became a regular holiday which is still celebrated some eight centuries later. Many other cultures throughout the galaxy have analogous celebrations."

"Tenira never had such a holiday, Commander Data," Arit said, "but maybe it's time to start a new tradition. Of course, I'm not sure whether the Shapers would appreciate a feast. But Captain, one year from today, you and your crew are invited to return to Mirrillon to join us in our thanksgiving celebration."

"We'd be honored to do so."

"Perhaps I'll cook you some fish, Picard," Arit said with a grin as a young female officer approached and whispered a relayed message to her. "Very good, Lieutenant. Captain, I've just been told your crew has beamed down the last supply shipment to the planet. I guess that means you'll be on your way."

Picard nodded. "We have a delayed mercy mission to complete, so we are in a bit of a hurry. We have already transmitted Mirrillon's application to the Federation Council. I am sure a positive response will be arriving with the first assistance teams."

"Well, Captain—there is no way we can possibly thank you and the *Enterprise* crew for all your help, and for extending the Federation's hand of welcome."

"We had a bit of a rocky start, but it was our pleasure, Captain Arit. Good luck to you—and to the Shapers. We'll be looking forward to your thanksgiving feast."

"So will we. Safe voyage, Picard."

"Welcome home, Arit. *Enterprise* out."

Arit faded from the viewer, replaced by an orbital view of the world henceforth to be known as Mirrillon. Riker joined Picard and Deanna Troi down in the starship's command well, easing into his seat at the captain's right. "Ready to leave orbit, sir."

But before Picard could respond, a multicolored cloud of energy materialized beneath the bridge's observation dome—with one golden sparkle inside, accompanied by the faint jangle of distant chimes.

:This is Ko, Captain Picard. The Shapers wish to thank you. We look forward to sharing the World—and to meeting other new life-forms from your Federation.:

"It is we who should thank you, Ko. Your willingness to embrace the unknown has given the Tenirans a second chance—and I'm sure your membership will enrich the Federation."

:Farewell, Captain.:

Then Ko was gone.

The bridge intercom beeped, followed by Beverly Crusher's voice. "Sickbay to Captain Picard."

"Picard here, Doctor."

"I just wanted to let you know we've conjured that promised medical miracle."

Picard's eyebrows rose in pleasant surprise. "Oh?"

"Yes. We just finished running our lab tests, and I think we've got a promising new treatment for ridmium poisoning. If it works on people even half as well as it does on the computer models, those injured workers at the Chezrani outpost have an excellent chance for full recovery."

"Ensign Crusher," Riker said, "set course for the Chezrani system."

Wesley's practiced fingers skipped across his console. "Course set, Commander."

"Warp factor seven, Ensign," Picard said, pointing ahead. "Engage."

As the *Enterprise* broke out of orbit, Riker leaned forward with a mischievous glimmer in his eye. "Data, there's something that bothered me about your Thanksgiving analogy."

The android swiveled slightly in his seat. "Oh? What was that, Commander?"

"You neglected to mention how American colonists and their descendants nearly exterminated the natives over the next couple of centuries. I've never known you to be any less than exhaustively complete in any factual report."

Data's eyebrows arched innocently. "I was, of course, aware of that unfortunate progression of historical events. But I did not believe the negative aspects of this particular account would serve a constructive purpose. So I delivered an edited version that seemed to be more . . . appropriate . . . for the occasion." He paused for a moment. "Was that judgment incorrect, sir?"

Riker's face spread into a smile. "Data, my friend, I couldn't have done it better myself." Then his expression turned pensive. "I just hope things work out better this time around. When you think about it, the Shapers and the Tenirans have even less in common than the American Indians and colonists did."

"That may be true, Will," Troi said, "but that could enhance the chances for harmonious coexistence. The Native Americans and the colonists wound up in competition for the same lands and resources. Here, because the Tenirans and the Shapers are so different, they may not step on each other's toes."

"Still," Riker said, "I wonder what it would be like to have the neighbors rearranging the *mountains* every thousand years."

"Unusual, to say the least," Picard said with a smile. "But the Shapers have promised to move mountains carefully, and the Tenirans have promised to be an appreciative audience."

"Audience, sir?" said Data.

"Yes, Data—providing one possible answer to an age-old debate."

"What debate is that, Captain?" Troi asked.

"Do sentient beings create for creation's sake, and self-satisfaction? Or do we create to communicate and share with others? Luckily for the Tenirans, *these* creators wanted to share."

With the satisfaction of a man who knew well the value of a smile from Lady Luck, Picard settled back into the command seat, turned to face the main screen, and enjoyed the view as his ship swept toward the stars.

About the Author

Perchance to Dream is Howard Weinstein's fifth "Star Trek" novel, following the previous best-sellers *Deep Domain* and *The Covenant of the Crown* from the original "Trek" series, and two other "Star Trek: The Next Generation" novels, *Exiles* and *Power Hungry*.

Since early 1991, Howard has also been the regular writer of the continuing adventures of Kirk, Spock, McCoy and the rest of the original "Star Trek" crew in the monthly comic-book series from DC Comics. (At home, he now speaks in word balloons.)

In 1974, as a 19-year-old University of Connecticut communications student, he became the youngest human (or alien, as far as we know) to write professionally for "Star Trek," selling *The Pirates of Orion* episode to NBC TV's Emmy-winning animated revival of the original series (now available on home video). A decade later, Howard was one of several writers consulted by Director Leonard Nimoy during his story-development idea hunt for *Star Trek IV: The Voyage Home,* and received a screen credit for his help.

In addition, Howard has written three original novels based on the NBC TV science fiction series *V*; articles, columns and reviews in *Starlog, The New York Times* and *Newsday;* and award-winning radio public service announcements. His slide shows have been seen by "Star Trek" convention audiences from coast to coast.

Yanked up by his New York roots, Howard was transplanted to Maryland where he lives with his wife Susan (who waters him daily) and their Welsh Corgi, Mail Order Annie.

Coming soon from Titan Books

STAR TREK®
THE NEXT GENERATION
SPARTACUS

by T L Mancour

Answering a distress call, the *Enterprise* finds a damaged alien vessel - the *Freedom* - crewed by a race known as the Vemlans. Their captain, Jerun, asks for assistance in repairing his ship - assistance Picard and the *Enterprise* are only too happy to provide. But once begun, their relief efforts are interrupted by the arrival of an entire fleet from Vemla, who claim that Jerun and his crew are escaped slaves - and their property!

As Jerun and his people plea for protection and the right to be free, Captain Picard is caught between the demands of his conscience and the dictates of the Prime Directive. And when the Vemlan fleet threatens to fight if the *Enterprise* doesn't stand aside, Picard must choose between the safety of his ship...and the annihilation of an entire race.

STAR TREK®
THE NEXT GENERATION

EXILES

For three centuries the people of Alaj and the people of
Etolos have been bitter enemies. However, when
crippling disasters strike both worlds, each planet
becomes the other's only hope of survival.

With time running out, Captain Picard and his crew
are called to negotiate a peaceful settlement and begin
rescue efforts. But some factions would rather see
both planets perish and will stop at nothing to
prevent peace.

Soon the *Enterprise* crew is caught up in a web of
intrigue and terrorism that culminates with an act
of ultimate revenge against both peoples - revenge
that will mean the destruction of two worlds and
the *Enterprise*!

THE COVENANT OF THE CROWN

An *Enterprise* shuttle is forced to crash-land in a violent storm on the barren planet of Sigma 1212. Spock, McCoy and Kailyn, heir to the Shaddan throne, survive the near disaster.

Pursued by primitive hunters and Klingon scouts, they must reach the mountains where the Shaddan crown is hidden and prove that Kailyn alone is the true heir to the throne.

If they fail, the door will open to Klingon takeover - and the galaxy's hope to live long and prosper will fall in the shadow of a cruel tyranny!

For a complete list of Star Trek publications, T-shirts and badges please send a SAE to Titan Books Mail Order, 19 Valentine Place, London, SE1 8QH. Please quote reference NG19.